Roberta Latow has be
Springfield, Massachusetts and New York City. She has
also been an international interior designer in the USA,
Europe, Africa and the Middle East, travelling extensively
to acquire arts, artefacts and handicrafts. Her sense of
adventure and her experiences on her travels have
enriched her writing; her fascination with heroic men
and women; how and why they create the lives they do
for themselves; the romantic and erotic core within – all
these themes are endlessly interesting to her, and form
the subjects and backgrounds for her novels.

Praise for Roberta Latow's novels:

'A wonderful storyteller. Her descriptive style is second
to none . . . astonishing sexual encounters . . . exotic
places, so real you can almost feel the hot sun on your
back . . . heroines we all wish we could be . . . irresistible'
Daily Express

'The fun of Latow's books is that they are genuinely
erotic . . . luxurious . . . full of fantasy. She has a better
imagination than most' *The Sunday Times*

'Passion on a super-Richter scale . . . Roberta Latow's
unique brand of erotic writing remains fresh and exciting'
Daily Telegraph

'Latow's writing is vibrant and vital. Her descriptions
emanate a confidence and boldness that is typical of her
characters . . . you can't help but be swept along by
them. A pleasure to read' *Books* magazine

Take Me Higher

Roberta Latow

HEADLINE

First published in 1999
by HEADLINE BOOK PUBLISHING

First published in paperback in 2000
by HEADLINE BOOK PUBLISHING

10 9 8 7 6 5 4 3 2 1

ISBN 0 7472 5958 5

Printed and bound in Great Britain by
Mackays of Chatham plc, Chatham, Kent

Typeset by CBS, Martlesham Heath, Ipswich, Suffolk

HEADLINE BOOK PUBLISHING
A division of the Hodder Headline Group
338 Euston Road
London NW1 3BH

www.headline.co.uk
www.hodderheadline.com

For
Vic Norman, Nick Mason, the Earl of Suffolk
and their magnificent flying machines

My sensual life
Rich and full of a rage to live
My passion for beauty in its various forms
Is to soar that little bit higher
Always that little bit higher

The Epic of Artimadon

Chapter 1

Diana George and her godson Keoki Richebourg heard the muffled hum of motors from somewhere out of sight over the Pacific Ocean. They both raised a hand to their forehead to shade their eyes as they scanned the sky, but all they could see was endless blue, clear of cloud, and the fiery red sun. A rose-coloured mist rolling in from the ocean hovered above the waves lapping on to the beach: a fringe of white froth on wet sand. Diana was aware of the unusual quiet. There was just one sound: waves as they broke, water rushing on to damp sand. Several hundred people, silent with anticipation, waited on balconies, terraces, roofs; they were standing two or three deep in front of Malibu beach houses and behind temporary barriers.

Diana felt her heart race as a droning sound broke the silence. She squeezed Keoki's hand then pointed to the sky. Fifteen vintage bi-planes: Gypsy, Tiger and Leopard Moths and Boeing Stearmans, handsome in their jewel colours, looked like huge prehistoric insects flying in formation. Coming in head on and at considerable speed,

1

the vintage planes brought murmurs of delight from the crowd, broad smiles to Diana's and Keoki's face. Excited, anticipation caused him to shout, 'Here comes my mom.'

Syrah Richebourg, Diana's best friend and Keoki's mother, was flying her Boeing Stearman in yet another of the day's aerobatics stunts: a kind of hopscotch while keeping in formation and never cutting speed. Just seconds before the bi-planes crossed the shoreline they pulled up sharply into a breathtakingly steep climb to miss the houses, made a barrel roll and flew out over the ocean from whence they came.

Diana and Keoki joined in the roar of approval and applause raised by the guests balancing their drinks: Tequila Sunrises, Margaritas, Mexican beer laced with lime. Children were licking ice cream cones and eating boxes of Crackerjacks.

Returning from a different direction, the bi-planes were flying one behind the other down the length of the cordoned-off beach. They peeled off in turn to land, taxi down the runway, line up and cut their motors. Syrah Richebourg's tangerine-coloured, double-winged Boeing Stearman was the last plane in the sky.

She flew it over the stretch of beach designated as an air strip with less bravado and more elegance than the others: an aerobatic ballet of pirouettes before she pulled out of a roll to bank and come in for a landing.

The double-winged craft raised the ocean spray in a spectacular finale. Diana was filled with a sense of joy for Syrah's triumph as she watched her friend finally

2

swing her plane away from the water's edge to come to a full stop in line with the others.

The crowd, exhilarated by her performance, hooted and hollered, and a twenty-four-piece sombrero-wearing Mariachi band struck up brassy Mexican sounds. A shoal of thousands of white and silver balloons floated upward, reaching into the sky. Several pilots dressed in the fun flying gear of the twenties and the thirties, worn by all dashing lovers of vintage planes and flying, gave Syrah and her tangerine Stearman a thumbs up and a broad smile.

Jack Bowater, standing in the crowd, watched Syrah's performance with his usual admiration for her love of life and adventure. His mind tripped back to the early hours of that very morning. He went over the scene meticulously, trying to come to terms with what had happened when Syrah, sitting on the edge of the bed pulling her jeans up over her legs, felt his arm slip around her waist and a hand caress her nakedness. Jack smiled to himself at the memory of how much he had enjoyed pulling her back to fall across his naked body, laughing.

'I thought you were asleep,' she told him.

'And so you could sneak away? Treat last night as you always do, nothing more than a one-night stand?' he asked her as he drew her on to the bed alongside him.

There had been no anger in Jack's voice. He and Syrah were too friendly, had too much fun together, were too honest with one another, for such an emotion to flare up

3

between them. It had been easy for Jack to set any indignation aside, he was not in love with her.

While still wriggling into her jeans, feeling replete after a night of sex and filled with a sense of vitality and excitement at the day ahead of her, Syrah had faced her lover and answered him, 'Let me go, Jack. We *are* casual sex, the exciting one-night stand. Last night was great, the erotic life always is, but it's no longer enough for me. I want more.'

'Love that comes with every beat of a man's heart, *and* sex unbound? A young girl's dream. Oh, come off it, Syrah. That's not you at all.' The facetious tone of his voice had been followed by nervous laugher.

'Laugh at me all you like, Jack, but grand passion that can happen between two people who are not afraid to commit themselves to each other *is* what I want. I'm suffering burn out from loving and being loved erotically and only for the moment. That kind of life is like quicksilver: it runs away with itself and in the end there's nothing left,' she had told him.

'You're serious about this!' was his shocked reply.

Syrah was slipping into a cream-coloured silk blouse with dramatic balloon sleeves, buttoning them tight to her wrist while gazing at her long-time on again, off again lover. 'Don't look at me askance, Jack, I've had a cracking good time. But affection, the momentary trip into sexual oblivion . . . great as that is, there has to be more for me. It's been a hell of a flight from real life and love and one I wouldn't have missed, but the time for escaping is over.

I wouldn't like my tombstone to read, "Here lies Syrah Richebourg, playgirl, who not so cleverly managed to live and die alone".'

'Why this sudden awakening, the yearning to change your life?' he asked, not bothering to hide the annoyance in his voice.

'It isn't so much that I want to change it as to add something more to it. It's not a very good feeling to realise that you've been short changing yourself in the love stakes, have been an under-achiever, too weak-willed to do anything about it. I want to leave more of a legacy than that for my son. This morning as I was watching the sun rise over the ocean I had a moment of total awareness, felt new strength in my heart and soul. Jack, be happy for me. I feel closer now to where I came from. And indeed I am my father's daughter, another Richebourg who wants to add something of value to our dynasty.'

Jack Bowater would miss her. She was quite a lady, adventurous, a cut above the other playgirls he dated. He and Syrah were gazing into each other's eyes when he told her, 'You're suddenly different.'

'Yes. It's quite inexplicable, a little frightening but thrilling,' she answered.

'I'll miss you. The old you.' There had been genuine sadness in his voice because he knew then it was over for them. She was a lady who would have what she wanted.

'Who knows? You might even like the new one better,' she had told him before kissing him farewell.

Jack knew that he would not like the new Syrah

Richebourg, whoever she might be. An emotion he was not prone to, fear of loss, took a grip on him then and he experienced a moment of regret for what he had not become in Syrah's life.

Syrah, still seated in her bi-plane, knew she would remember this particular demonstration and the landing on the beach in Malibu as the beginning of the end of her life, her whole world, as she had always known it.

She removed her flying goggles, unbuckled the chin strap of her leather cap and pulled it off. A mass of auburn hair tumbled on to her shoulders to frame her beautiful face. She shook it out and ran her fingers through it. The green eyes flashed with excitement, the wry smile displayed satisfaction for an inspired fly over and declared her to the crowd as naturally happy-go-lucky, a thrill seeker and adventurer. Heaving herself from the rear cockpit of the plane, she vigorously waved the white silk scarf she had pulled from round her neck.

Syrah was not waving to the crowd or to her peers but to her handsome, exotic-looking child and her best friend, Diana George. The boy was Syrah's nine-year-old illegitimate son, issue of a passionate love affair with an Hawaiian. She watched the two racing across the sand towards her and, lagging behind, her faithful housekeeper, Melba Morissey.

'Mom, Mom, you were fantastic!' shouted Keoki, beaming as he sprinted past Diana, his cap flying off his head.

She threw her head back and laughed. How she loved her son, adored his sweetness, his incredible capacity for happiness. While still making a dash for his mother, Keoki called out as he attempted to pass two of the pilots standing next to a Leopard Moth, 'Hi, Vic! Hi, Nick!'

The two men caught the boy, hoisted him on to their shoulders and carried him over to Syrah's plane as if he were the star of the day instead of his mother.

Syrah, looking glamorous in her black leather jump suit, hopped down from her plane to hug her son, tousle his hair and greet her friends.

She felt happy. The feeling had started at dawn that morning when she'd walked away from Jack, somehow changed by a moment of awareness. And the day just kept getting better. The air show was a triumph thanks to more than thirty pilots who had flown their vintage planes in from far-flung places to be there and participate in the show. They had been daring and inspirational. From the moment of their arrival earlier in the day they had created an atmosphere that was electric and fun. The air even now, late in the day, was still crackling with it. This sense of fun, all different sorts of adventure and thrills, made up a great part of Syrah and Keoki Richebourg's lifestyle.

Diana arrived, and not far behind her a huffing and puffing Melba, badly out of breath. There were pats on backs, hugs and kisses for Syrah, comments about the display and praise for a spectacular turn out on behalf of the California Save the Children Fund.

Syrah felt high with happiness, delighted that she had

everyone she loved around her except for Ethan Richebourg, her father, the most important man in her life. It was he who would instinctively understand that a fundamental change was about to take over her life. Ethan loved her and would help her to realise her new dream, she knew. Syrah couldn't help but smile; she had always been his child of many dreams and he had always supported her in them. Knowing that Ethan had wanted to be there but had been prevented by a long-standing business engagement did not stop her from gazing around hopefully. He was all that was missing to make her day perfect.

The show now over, the crowd, who had paid five-hundred dollars a ticket to the charity for a finger-food luncheon of California and Mexican cuisine, which included whole roasted pigs, lambs over charcoal pits dug in the sand, mountains of strawberries capped with whipped cream and drizzled with Vermont maple syrup, and an all-day air display, began to thin out.

Syrah and her friends were walking towards the grandstand where the corporate and private patrons, donating a hundred thousand dollars and upwards, had been seated when they were joined by Ira Rudman, one of the charity's more important sponsors. He was, in fact, the man who had organised the event down to the last detail, including dealing with the authorities and Malibu residents to gain permission to close off and prepare a section of the beach for a runway and create a strip for the scores of private planes that had flown in conveying guests. It was he who had cajoled a number of beach house owners into opening their houses to selected VIP guests: a Hollywood contingent of stars, moguls, writers, producers, actors, movie people both old and young who had turned out to support the charity and for a fun day where they and their families might be seen but were not the centre of attraction. The mega-rich Californian businessmen and politicians who wheeled and dealed for the success and glory of the state were there too in force.

Ira went directly to Syrah and slipped his arm through hers. He beamed down at her with all the charm and rugged good looks that had captured Diana George's heart and made them live-in lovers for so many years. Syrah felt the power of Ira's sexual charisma and as usual automatically rejected any thought of a liaison, brief or otherwise, with him. She had after all been fending off Ira's erotic hunger for her for years.

Having to remain not only civil but friendly towards him for Diana's sake had not been easy but very necessary since she had no intention of losing her best friend because of a man.

The way Ira stroked her hair, fawning over her in front of Diana, Keoki and her friends, embarrassed Syrah. She made an attempt to separate herself from him, but in vain. He tightened his grip on her arm. Syrah understood only too well the attraction he had for women. He was handsome and sexy, intelligent, a man who adored women and knew how to flatter them, make them feel marvellous about themselves and about loving him. He could be generous and kind when he wanted to be, amusing, a powerful personality who knew how to get what he wanted and was ruthless in the pursuit of his goals. But looking at him served only as a reminder to Syrah that the love of a good man and true commitment, not sex with a successful, powerful cad who treated women like chattels, was what she must find now.

She had always recognised the shark in Ira but never more so than she did while he held her in his grip. She saw the danger in his eyes: sensuous dark pools; manipulative, corrupting eyes. She suddenly felt her own strength. This was *her* day, *her* success, and though he had helped make it happen for her those soulful eyes, brought to bear on her to enslave her to him, very nearly made her laugh. Ira's eyes might as well have been shut, for they had no effect on her. Diana was through with Ira. *Ipso facto* Syrah no longer needed to play the friendship game with him. He was one of the people she would happily leave behind now that she had plans to forge ahead, seeking a new and more meaningful place for herself in the sun. The future opened before her, new and fresh and exciting. She could hardly wait to talk her new plans over with her son, her father – who would be delighted at this new turn in her life – and of course with Diana. She and her friend told each other everything.

Ira caressed her shoulder and Syrah, not wanting to make a scene, did not pull away but glared disapprovingly at him.

'Remember me? I'm the man who made your moment

of glory possible,' he reminded her.

What audacity! The velvet trap. How good Ira was at setting it, thought Syrah. She had seen him do it to others so many times and yet she hadn't seen the one he had been setting for her.

Now it all flashed back to her: how with some people, at their moment of glory, he pulled the rug out from under them and they fell from the very heights he had raised them to. Most of them were never able to recover themselves again, their egos damaged beyond repair. With others he allowed them their moment and then appeared, ready and waiting for the pay-off.

Syrah laughed in his face. He had found her weakness: an ego that wanted a little inflating, a desire to arrange a spectacular air show. Now *she* was supposedly in his debt and *he* was blatant about collecting his dues. But not this time, Ira, and not this girl, she told herself.

He had approached her with an offer she could not refuse: organising, gratis, air shows on a small scale for charitable causes was her contribution to society, her way of giving a little something back for her pampered and privileged life. She wanted this opportunity to plan an air show on a grand scale and grabbed it without a second thought because of the support and co-operation she knew Ira would give it. He was not a man for half measures.

Now he lifted Syrah off the sand and swung her around several times. 'You did it! What a show you pulled together. I'm eternally grateful to you. People are raving about the event and large donations are pouring in from the grandstand brigade.'

Syrah was laughing and full of joy at her success. The object of the exercise, after all, had been to raise several million dollars for the less fortunate children of California. Children from poverty-stricken, one-parent homes; abandoned babies and toddlers; the mentally handicapped. She begged Ira to put her down and he did but not before he'd kissed her first on one cheek then the other. The kisses appeared innocent enough but the way he held her, the manner in which his hands roamed over the skin-tight leather of her flying suit, was embarrassing to her. It happened and was over so quickly she was certain no one else had seen his moment of lasciviousness. Syrah very nearly thought she'd imagined more than had really happened. He was so cunning! She stiffened with outrage. Was that to be the pay-off he demanded, a sexual liaison?

Diana had missed nothing of what was going on between Ira and Syrah. She felt quite sick, not jealous but angry with Ira. The joy she had been feeling all day seemed to drain away. She and Ira were estranged – the pain and humiliation he had been causing her for years could no longer be borne. He had expected her to grin and bear his infidelities because he still wanted Diana in his life and home. He loved her more than he had ever loved any other woman and had expected that to be enough for her. Now they were barely on speaking terms because she had finally walked out on him.

Diana managed to keep her emotions under control when he swung away from Syrah to greet her. He took a lock of her hair, held it in his fingertips and, smiling at her, told her: 'Diana, looking cool and beautiful as always. I miss you.'

Those years of loving him: the wonder and the misery; the womanising and broken promises; his brilliant ruthless wheeling and dealing in business; his generosity and love for her, all flashed through her mind. He had been the most exciting man she had ever known, the only one she had ever lived with and wanted to marry. Diana wanted to ask, 'I wonder if that's true, Ira?' but thought better of it. She remained silent.

'No comment?' he asked.

'Merely congratulations. What a great day you have given the fund.'

The cold look in his eyes for Diana, the ice that had been in his voice while talking to her, melted away as he turned on his heel to give all his attention once more to Syrah. 'Let's go,' he told her, slipping his arm through hers.

Feeling her friend's pain, she was reluctant to go anywhere with him. However, believing herself obliged to go to the dinner party arranged at Ira's beach house for donors, she felt she had little choice but to accompany him.

Removing his arm from hers, Syrah took Diana and Keoki aside and told them, 'As one of the organisers of this event, I'm committed to this evening at Ira's house. I have all these fly boys to thank for coming out for me, and, well, those major contributors to the fund deserve some thanks too. But you know who I'd rather be with.'

Diana, having recovered herself, assured Syrah. 'We know. Go and have a great time, you deserve it. Keoki and I have our evening planned: your house, pizza and chocolate milkshakes, TV, Scrabble, then bed.'

Syrah kissed her son and watched him and Diana walk off down the beach towards her house, Melba straggling behind. She turned to Ira and, slipping her arm through his, told him, 'You can be so good and generous – and such a shit at the same time. Must you tease Diana with that intimate caressing of her hair, that sexy, husky, just a little desperate "I miss you", accompanied by a vulnerable look, when you know how she's struggling to get over you?

'But that's you all over, isn't it? Always give the ladies in love with you a little hope, just enough so they can never really dump you. That calculated iciness in your voice that they can't bear . . . oh, you can be cruel! It works on women in love, makes them work harder at loving you, makes them believe there is something more they can do, one little thing and you're theirs forever. How I hate men like you who manipulate women! If I had been in Diana's shoes just now and had a gun, I'd have shot you dead, you bastard.'

Syrah wrenched her arm free from his grasp and gave him a withering look. She had no intention of allowing her fury with him to ruin her day. Having expressed her feelings, she had no need to consider him further. She could deal with Ira.

He grabbed her by the arm and, holding it firmly, told her, 'I believe you get off on the idea that you would have, but you wouldn't, you know. The sexual attraction we feel towards each other stops you. I'm on to you, Syrah. It's not loyalty to Diana or fear that she will discover how much we lust after each other that holds you back. It's that you're afraid once you've discovered how great sex between us could be that you might fall in love with me. And you don't do that – fall in love with your lovers – not since Keoki's father. You fuck your lovers and leave them. You and I are a lot alike except that I'm not afraid to fall in love. At least I loved Diana. Remember, it was she who walked out on our life together, I never sent her packing.'

'Let go of my arm, you're hurting me, Ira,' she told him, anger sparkling in her eyes.

He loosened his grip, very much aware that Syrah's attraction to him and her constant rejection of his overtures to her had created a love-hate tension between them that had over the years become an obsession for Ira. He wanted to possess Syrah: body, soul, and all she represented – an adventurous and exciting nature, social standing, inherited wealth, a powerful and respected family name. Everything he himself had not been born to.

'Sorry, I didn't mean to hurt you or to be so candid. I thought we had become friends?'

'Friends of a sort. But you won't accept that. You'll never accept that that's all we'll ever be. I know you, Ira.

You're thinking: "I'll have her, one way or another. I'll take possession of her." But you won't, you know.'

She smiled at him and thought, It's like swimming with the sharks.

'We'll see. Remember, the opera's not over until the fat lady sings, Syrah.'

She could not help but laugh then and when she stopped told him, 'You're incorrigible!'

'Well, at least you got that right.'

Dusk was fast approaching, another kind of magic at Malibu made even more so by the line of planes revving motors and taking off one after the other, guests flying home while they still had the light. None of the excitement seemed to be waning from the day. The very air they breathed felt as if charged with adrenaline. Intoxicated with it and still playing their usual game of love-hate flirtation, Syrah and Ira approached his house. It was large and impressive, considered very grand even by the grandest of Malibu standards. The interior was elegant with his collections of Ming and Tang Dynasty artefacts; eclectic in the way the contemporary paintings – Jim Dine and Warhol, a superb collection of Rothko and Hans Hoffman, Clifford Still, Picasso and Matisse – lived at ease with a Poussin among French commodes, Bergère chairs and contemporary furniture covered in cream-coloured suede.

Syrah could see people milling around the reception rooms, through the open two-storey high French doors. She could hear the faint sound of music: a Debussy duet.

It reminded her of the innumerable times over the years that she had enjoyed Ira and Diana's hospitality here, those days when they were a three or foursome (Syrah was a much sought after date among eligible men). She and Diana, when she was not filming or in a play, had lived a happy-go-lucky existence and had been naive about Ira and how different their ideas were from his on the subject of love and friendship. It had taken years for Syrah to understand that her friend's lover was a cad and could also be a dangerous man if thwarted.

Once in the house they were swept up by the guests who had arrived before them: men in black tie and dress suits, women beautiful in stunning gowns and dazzling jewels. There were mega-wealthy Californian wives, lovers and mistresses, a smattering of Hollywood starlets, and handsome bachelors ranging from the north to the south of the state, plus the odd South American polo player, Italian count or English earl for added interest and colour. The flying contingency that had come out for the display were yet to arrive but even without them there was a buzz going that guaranteed a terrific evening ahead.

Syrah rose to the occasion and warmly greeted several Napa Valley friends of her father's, wine barons like Ethan Richebourg and women who had known her since she was a child, fondly considering her a wayward daughter. They all descended on her with praise for her part in the day. A glass of champagne and several miniature blinis later she was shepherded away by Ira, already bathed and changed into his evening clothes and looking particularly handsome and happy. He took her up the stairs to his bedroom. There, as planned, she found her evening clothes laid out across the bed; she had sent along her dressing case earlier in the day with Melba.

Without a word to her host, and with not a moment's hesitation, she swept from bedroom to bathroom, closed the door and locked it. She could hear Ira's laughter through the door. Syrah smiled. It did so amuse her to out-fox his lust. Twisting a towel round her head to protect her hair from the steam, she ran the bath and took her time luxuriating in the almond-scented bath water.

When Syrah emerged, wrapped in a terry-cloth robe, and sat in one of the arm chairs to make up her face and brush her hair, Ira was gone, just as she'd thought he would be. The mischievous, flirtatious side of her nature was just a little disappointed nevertheless.

On went sheer black stockings and high-heeled black satin sandals. She slipped into a halter top, bias-cut, plum-coloured silk taffeta evening dress.

All her attention was concentrated on doing up the clasp at the back of her neck. She didn't hear Ira slip into the room and only knew he was there when he stepped up behind her and placed a kiss on the small of her naked back, running a pointed tongue down over the swell of her flesh before he pulled up the zip.

Her heart was pounding with sensual excitement but that did not stop Syrah from pulling away from him immediately. 'Never, Ira!' she told him as she swung around to confront him.

'Smart women never say never,' he told her as he walked around her.

Her dress was bare-backed to just below the waist. He caressed her naked flesh and then, before she realised what was happening, pulled her back against him and held her tight. A knock at the bedroom door snapped her back to the reality of her situation.

She released herself from his embrace and told him, 'I repeat, never! Maybe you're wrong. Maybe it's the *very* smart women who know how to say words like "never" and "no" to men like you, Ira. Men who profess to love one woman and want to sate their appetites with another for love of conquest and nothing else.'

The wry smile on his lips and his silence as he walked across the room to open the door annoyed her. It was at that moment that she realised Ira Rudman would never give up on her. She had been deluding herself that she could swim with a shark like him.

Syrah was standing in front of the long mirror. Making last adjustments to her gown she saw Ira and his houseman, Roberts, reflected in it at the open door. The two men were whispering, both looking very serious indeed. A terrible sense of dread came over her. She placed the palm of her hand over her heart and walked to the door where the men were standing.

'Is something wrong?' she asked.

'Diana and Keoki are waiting at the front door, insisting on seeing you immediately, Syrah,' answered Ira.

She felt that something must be very wrong for Diana and her son to be there at all and fled from the room without another word. Her feeling of foreboding was increased tenfold as she dashed down the stairs and through the hall. The party, in full swing now with laughter and music – two pianos and several artists singing Sondheim songs from *Follies* – suddenly seemed like a scene from a nightmare. Several people tried to stop her with congratulations on the air display that afternoon. Her escort for the evening, Diego Juarez, a famous South American polo player who was a close friend and sometime lover, a man who had much in common with Syrah since he was as much a playboy as she was a playgirl and came from as important a wine family as she did, recognised something was wrong when she passed him by without a word. He followed her.

She flung open the front door to find Keoki and Diana standing there just as Ira had said. The look of distress on her son's face told it all. She patted his head and kissed him several times. With tears in her eyes she addressed Diana. 'It's my father, isn't it? Something's happened to Ethan.'

'Pops is very sick, Mom. Diana says we can be upset but we have to be strong, for Pop's sake. But I don't feel very strong,' Keoki faltered.

Syrah placed an arm round her son and pulled him against her to comfort him. By this time Ira and Diego were at her side. Diego, who had known Keoki since he was a baby, took him from Syrah and walked him away, talking to him in a soothing voice. Diego had known and respected Ethan all his life; his father was one of Ethan's best friends. The news was distressing for him too. Ethan had been more than a good friend to him when Diego had inherited the family vineyards and winery in his native Chile.

With Keoki out of earshot, Diana was able to fill in the details. 'Your brother Caleb called. Ethan's had a stroke and the prognosis is very bad. It's just a matter of time, a very short time.'

Syrah felt her whole world crashing down around her. Her father was her greatest friend: a man of charm and accomplishment whom she respected and admired. Though disapproving of the playgirl life she had chosen away from the family winery in the Napa Valley, he had supported her right to live as she wanted to and loved her for it. Fear gripped her. She had never even considered a life without her father.

'You must get a grip on yourself, Syrah. Ethan is calling for you – there's no time to lose. I've brought you a change of clothes.'

'You're right,' she answered mechanically.

'I'll charter you a plane,' offered Ira.

'No. Thanks, but it will be faster if you get one of the fly boys to refuel my plane and get it ready for take off. Ira, please tell the men controlling air traffic down on the runway to get me at the head of the queue. I'll be down as soon as I change. Diana, please call Caleb and ask him to tell my father that Keoki and I are on the way. He's to have the lights on the air strip turned on and a car waiting to take me up to the house.'

Diego and Keoki overheard the last few words as they approached Syrah. Diego immediately offered, 'I think you're under enough stress, I'll fly you.'

'Thanks, but I can get more out of the Stearman and get us there faster if I fly it.'

'I don't think you should make this flight alone, Syrah,' Ira cautioned.

'Oh, do shut up, Ira, she won't be alone – I'm going with her,' Diana told him, barely able to conceal the anxiety in her voice.

There was relief on Syrah's face and gratitude in her eyes as she swiftly hugged her friend before she dashed back to Ira's bedroom to climb once more into her flying suit.

They took off from Malibu for the Richebourg-Conti vineyard in the Napa Valley while the sun still hovered over the horizon. Syrah was at the controls, Keoki crammed with Diana in the forward seat of the two-seater bi-plane.

Chapter 2

On the ground Syrah had been traumatised by fear at the prospect of losing her father but had kept herself under a semblance of control so as not to frighten her son. Up in the air, in the vast emptiness and silence except for the sound of the Stearman's motor, her courage returned. She could see things more clearly, accept the realities of life more easily when she was flying. It had something to do with looking down from space and seeing the smallness of the earth. The tumult of life vanished in minutes. How insignificant and vulnerable man really was in the greater context of the world and existence.

Chased by the coming of night, flying against time with the wind in her face, reaching her father was all Syrah cared about. She imagined herself holding his hand and kissing his forehead, telling him how much she loved him and that together they would fight for his life. If there were to be a death tonight, it would not be Ethan's. He would never leave her without saying goodbye. The grim reaper would have to wait for another day. No less distressed, she at least for the moment conquered her fear of what she might have to face: the reality of Ethan's situation and consequently her own.

Syrah considered Château Richebourg-Conti, its vineyards and winery that were her home, the roots from whence she sprung. That was the way Ethan had always made her feel in spite of her deserting it, except for Christmas, other holidays and flying visits to be with her father. A terrifying thought took hold of her then and tears came to her eyes, the wind spreading them across her cheeks. She was virtually estranged from her brother Caleb, his wife Paula and their children. What if Ethan did die? What if she, Caleb and his wife did not come together in their grief? She would then be made unwelcome at Richebourg-Conti, sent away from the family home, the haven that had always been there for her. Her brother and sister-in-law, who only just tolerated Syrah and were no more than stiffly civil to Keoki because Ethan demanded it would surely cut them both out of their lives and what ought to be Keoki's heritage. The very thought made Syrah feel sick at heart. She blanked it from her mind and concentrated on piloting her craft.

There were some blessings to this flight to the Valley: it was a warm night and they were experiencing a longer than usual sunset, the wind was behind them all the way and they were able to fly relatively low. Santa Barbara was behind them, Monterey could be made before dark, but it would be night and off in the distance San Francisco would be aglow with lights and looking like millions of stars had fallen from a galaxy as they made for Napa and then home to Richebourg-Conti.

Home: the Richebourg-Conti vineyard and château that she had always loved but had turned her back on because of a craving to live in a wider world. Syrah was suddenly aware that if her father did indeed die, Richebourg-Conti would no longer be her home.

The thought affected her profoundly. Suddenly she understood what a tremendous loss that would be for her. She had been living too fast and thrilling a life, one day at a time, to sit down and think about her attachment to Richebourg-Conti before this. It was a part of her ancestry, always there for her, as sure as there was a moon and a sun to guide her in life. Syrah had never thought before what would happen to Richebourg-Conti without Ethan. He *was* Richebourg-Conti, as his father and his grandfather before him, and so many generations of Richebourgs before them, had been.

The vineyards without Ethan there . . . A tremendous sense of foreboding came over Syrah. Caleb trying to step into their father's shoes? Everything would change then, nothing would be the same for Richebourg-Conti. The idea was so overwhelming to her that it didn't even occur to Syrah that with Ethan's death everything else might change for her: the loss of fatherly and family love would leave her adrift and alone except for Keoki. The security of having Richebourg-Conti as the backbone of her life would be lost to her. And financial security? How long before that was cut off too?

25

She had never before appreciated that those things were the props on which she had built her life. With those sturdy foundations knocked away from beneath her, where would she be? Fallen, destroyed! How would she and Keoki survive? Sheer terror gripped her then. Syrah's confidence vanished. It was gone as if it had never existed. Her head throbbed with pain, her mouth went dry. The plane went into a dive. She gripped the Stearman's controls as hard as she could until her fingernails cut into the palms of her hands and she pulled the plane up. The pain brought her back to the task at hand: getting to Richebourg-Conti safely and as fast as possible so as to be with Ethan. Fear would have to wait. So would the future and her fate.

Ethan had installed a beacon on the conical roof of one of the towers of Château Richebourg-Conti. The switch for both the beacon and the low-level lights marking out the grass air strip could be pressed in the library. The usual form was that Syrah would call in to announce her estimated arrival time. The beacon on, she would buzz the house and the lights to the air strip would be switched on. Normally by the time she had landed, Ethan or Mr Wang, the *major domo* who ran the château and most of her father's private life, would be at the air strip having driven down from the house.

But these were not normal times at Richebourg-Conti, Syrah could see that even from the air: the beacon was on and every window in the house aglow with lamplight. As she flew low to buzz the house she could see people with flashlights on the tree-lined drive to the house, some carrying flowers. The terrace and steps to the front door were now nothing more than a narrow path flanked by flowers. At the end of the three-quarter-mile-long drive the gates stood open and several cars were parked there, presumably belonging to the winery and vineyard workers who were paying their respects with get well floral tributes.

That view of things was to bring home to Syrah just how bad things were and what a sad loss Ethan's passing would be to so many people. No matter how strong she was being, how tightly she was holding herself under control, she was aware that her sense of self had deserted her. She was adrift, in pain and fear, and yet none of that mattered. Only her love for her father and surrounding him with that love did.

The lights sprang to life to either side of the air strip which was only a short drive from the house – a signal to her to swallow her pain and control her emotions, not only for her son's sake but her father's as well. She had to take on Ethan's strength now, fight for him and his life, give him the support he had always given her so as to help him until, hopefully, he was well enough to take control of his own life and recovery.

She circled the air field only once and set the plane down in a perfect landing. She cut the engine and, feeling quite drained of all emotions as well as exhausted by the flight, took several deep breaths as she watched a car's headlights speeding across the field towards the bi-plane.

'You all right?' she shouted to Diana and Keoki.

'OK, Mom.'

'Diana?'

'Nothing worse than windswept and a little cramped. We're just fine,' she called back from the open forward seat of the plane.

The propeller was moving as if in slow motion now, a signal for Diana and Keoki to make a move. Diana pulled off the scarf tied around the hat she was wearing, removed the hat and shook out her hair. Hugging Keoki to her, she reminded him, 'Remember, we're going to stick together while we're here and let your mom tend to your grandfather. Anything you want or need, you ask me or Mr Wang. Low profiles until Syrah tells us what's happening and when you can see your grandfather. No tears, no demands. You need to do this for your mom and granddad.'

With that she kissed the boy she loved almost as much as if he were her own, the child she had always wanted from Ira, and combed his hair by running her fingers through it.

'I'm not a baby, Diana. I understood all that when you told me before we climbed aboard in Malibu.'

Baby or not, she could not help but notice the tremor in his voice, the fear and sadness in his eyes. Then he kissed her briefly on the cheek and told her, 'You'd better comb your hair and maybe put on some lipstick, we want to look as if we're together, don't we? Not let our side down. You're an actress, it's expected of you to look glamorous even when you're sad.'

Diana very nearly burst into tears of pride at her godson's behaviour. How long had he known that without Ethan the château might be nothing more for him than an enemy camp? Sometimes nine years old going on eighteen, she told herself.

The three of them were on the ground only a minute or two before Caleb arrived driving Ethan's Second World War army jeep, the top down. It was a blow for Syrah to see her brother driving the jeep; no one but Ethan drove that vehicle usually. Everyone in the Valley knew that. There seemed to be three of them gazing with sadness and astonishment at Caleb, something cruel about his choice of transportation, taking the jeep even before Ethan was dead. Especially since it was a known fact he didn't even like it.

Seeing Caleb already trying to step into her father's shoes turned Syrah's fear to anger. Visions of the past flashed before her eyes: she and Ethan arm-in-arm arriving at the winery; with nothing more than a look her father demanding and receiving at least cordiality, if nothing more, for her from his son and daughter-in-law. The Christmas picture taken every year: Ethan flanked by his daughter, son and daughter-in-law looking every inch the autocrat with a smile in his eyes, full of pride in himself and his family. The resentment on Caleb and Paula's faces because Ethan controlled the Richebourg-Conti vineyards and winery and was one of the most respected names in the industry, producing one of the most prestigious and sought after wines to come out of the Napa Valley, was clearly visible. They wanted everything Ethan represented, all he had achieved.

Syrah bit into her lower lip, attempting to control her temper. Looking at her brother now she could not help but wonder what had happened to the sweet child she had grown up with who once had loved and cared for her. She thought now of that terrible confrontation she had had with him and Paula when she was pregnant with Keoki. She had wanted them to love and accept her, be her family. She had approached them, determined to talk out the problems they had with one another.

One afternoon when she was making a visit to the château she found herself alone with them in the garden. Remembering it now sent a shiver down her spine. She had just come out with it, 'Caleb, why do you and Paula feel such hostility towards me? The not-so-subtle barbs you're constantly throwing at me lead me to believe it stems from Ethan's love for me and his acceptance of my lifestyle. Tell me that's not true?'

Paula had replied, 'Of course it's true! As is our resentment over the vast sums of money you've received over the years from Richebourg-Conti. Both Caleb and I work for the family vineyard and winery, we earn the money Ethan squanders on you! Whatever Syrah wants, Syrah gets! Not Caleb. Diversifying Richebourg-Conti's holdings in the business schemes we put to Ethan might better all our lives. But, oh, no. Always the same excuse: Richebourg-Conti's business is the grape, the Richebourgs are wine people to the depths of their soul and care for nothing but the wine industry. Excuses! We know it's really Ethan's favouritism for you that blinds him.'

Caleb's words when he interrupted his wife's diatribe rang now in Syrah's ears as she faced her brother. 'Paula and I love Ethan as much as you do, Syrah, in spite of the way he undermines our authority and keeps us from realising our potential. But does he love and support *us*? Maybe, in things that don't really matter to us. And nowhere near the way he lavishes affection and money on you. In our eyes *he's* guilty of favouritism and *your* selfish greed fans the flame. You're a spoiled little bitch, Syrah. Always have been, always will be.'

But that confrontation was many years ago, she desperately told herself now. As Caleb leaped from the jeep to walk towards Syrah, he could see what she and Diana were thinking by the look that passed between the two women. He rather enjoyed their hesitation to say anything about his driving the jeep and experienced a cheap sense of triumph in showing them that he was in control of things. It was a clever cover-up for the emotional turmoil in his head and his heart. The fact was that Caleb and Paula were just as traumatised by Ethan's illness as Syrah was, but for different reasons.

They were shocked that in a matter of hours, days at the most, he would be dead and gone forever and *they* would at last be in control of all of Richebourg-Conti. The years of dreaming, plotting and scheming to wrench control away from Ethan, the entrenched resentment, the peculiar sort of love-hatred they felt for his father, were at last over. Caleb's time had come. The heir to the Richebourg-Conti throne would soon be wearing the crown he and Paula had worked so hard to take over. Now that he had what he wanted Caleb could afford to love his father as he had not done since he was a boy.

Sister and brother shook hands, Caleb patted Keoki on the head and greeted Diana cordially. 'How's Dad, Caleb?' asked Syrah, a tremor of emotion in her voice.

Although he was no less resentful of his sister and what Ethan's indulgence towards her had cost him, he was nevertheless relieved that she was there to share the burden.

'He's in a shocking state but still with us, so be prepared and try and conceal your distress. Once Dad regained consciousness and could make himself understood he had only one thing to say: "Syrah". He's been repeating your name constantly. Nothing can calm him. There'll be no peace for him or anyone in the house until you're at his bedside. It's as if all he's living for is to have one last look at you. It's unnerving and heartbreaking.'

They were all clambering into the jeep, Syrah struggling to hold back sobs of anguish as she asked, 'When did Dad have his stroke?'

'Let's talk after you've seen him.'

They sped from the air strip to the house. The three new arrivals, still in their fleece-lined leather flying jackets, clung on tight to iron hand grips as they were bounced about roughly in that dreaded silence that only accompanies the coming of death.

Keoki broke down in floods of tears as he'd hoped he would not when they walked up the main staircase to the house, flanked solidly by masses of flowers. He clung to Syrah who was trying to reassure him that Ethan was still with them.

In the hall they were met by Mr Wang. The old retainer and Syrah hugged each other but said nothing. They were too choked by emotion for Mr Wang to do anything else but help her off with her jacket. It was then that Paula emerged from the library.

'Diana, Keoki, Mr Wang will show you to your rooms. I'm sure you will want to freshen up. Why don't you come into the library, Syrah, and we'll put you in the picture?'

'That can wait, Paula – I want to see my father before anything else. I would, however, be grateful if you could give Keoki and Diana something warm to drink, it's been a long flight.' With that she took the stairs two at a time and went directly to her father's room.

Syrah had to take several deep breaths before gently knocking on the door. She had no preconceived idea of what to expect, having not taken in Caleb's warning. On entering the bedroom her knees nearly buckled under her. Ethan's room was large and lovely with a series of windows offering a view of the garden and vineyards for as far as the eye could see. But the terraces of vines rising towards the mountains on one side and far off in to the distance towards the thin ribbon of blue that was the Pacific Ocean on the other, seemed to be visible no longer.

It had always been a rich room, sensuous in its masculine ambience. The French eighteenth-century cherrywood panelling was hung with French Napoleonic engravings, an Ingres oil of a reclining nude odalisque wearing a blue satin turban wound round her head, a David and a Delacroix. The deep, rich, egg-yolk yellow silk damask draperies tied back with massive period silk tassels she had played with as a child; the four-poster canopied bed draped in deep magenta and lined in amethyst paper taffeta; the soft and comforting light that filtered through cream-coloured silk shades on lamps whose bases were handsome period Chinese wine jars; all of this receded now to a point where it could hardly be seen for hospital apparatus: life support systems, oxygen tanks, the flashing and beeping of what little life Ethan had in him echoing from machines. Two nurses in crisp white uniforms moved around the room, another sitting by Ethan. A doctor stood at the far side of the bed making notes on a small pad.

Syrah felt a hand on her shoulder and then Caleb's arm went around her to steady her. The room was silent except for the monitors' sounds and a faint gravelly noise: her father struggling to say 'Syrah'.

He managed it a second and a third time before Caleb told her, 'If he stops calling for you once he sees you it will be a blessing for him as well as for us. I can't bear to see him so weak, so desperate. Neither can Paula. I tried to warn you to prepare yourself, hang on for his sake.'

'He's not delirious, you know. Just determined to survive long enough to see you. Maybe now you're here he can rest. That ceaseless calling for you has unnerved us all. I'm so relieved you're here to stop it.' The last was from Paula who had arrived to stand with them.

Syrah left them standing at the door. She walked directly to the bed and saw her father properly for the first time. He was propped up against linen pillows trimmed with ecru-coloured lace and in fact looked far better than she had expected him to. He was as handsome as he had been when she had seen him a week before except that there was no vitality left in his face. His eyes were devoid of light, passion, love for life and laughter; even the intelligence that had always shown in them was dimmed. She thought her heart would break as she watched him form his lips once more to call her name.

She approached the nurse who was sitting in a chair next to the bed. The woman was holding Ethan's hand in hers and stroking it. She placed his hand gently on the white linen coverlet, rose from the chair and stepped aside. Syrah bent over the bed and kissed her father on the forehead, one cheek and then the other, took his hand and squeezed it. He blinked at her and stopped calling her name, closed his eyes and issued a sigh of relief.

All the colour drained from her face.

'He's very tired, has little strength. He's just dozed off, he does that often.'

Syrah very nearly collapsed into the chair and took her father's hand in hers. She leaned forward and kissed it before she turned to the nurse. 'I'm Syrah.'

'I'm Miss Turtle. The nurse standing with the doctor is Mrs Crumb and my other colleague is Miss Sanchez. It's good you're here. Don't expect too much. Keep talking to Mr Richebourg, that's important, and hold his hand as you're doing now. He needs life around him and love.' Then she walked away, leaving father and daughter together.

After several minutes the doctor Syrah had known all her life approached her. He patted her on the shoulder, checked the machines monitoring his patient, then asked to have a private word with her.

Together they walked to the windows. 'Ethan will rest more comfortably now that you're here, Syrah. He might even rally somewhat, but you mustn't raise your hopes. I doubt he can sustain even a partial recovery. I'm sorry.'

'Do you think he understands how ill he is?'

'His mind isn't addled, just slower. He can speak when he has the strength and wants to, and at least make himself understood. But it's best to remember that every word he utters is a tremendous struggle for him. You should try to do most of the talking, Syrah. Ethan is partially paralysed down his left side.

'I think you ought to know that he left a copy of a letter with me years ago – the original is lodged with his attorney. He wants not to be kept alive on a life support machine and to die with as much dignity as is possible. If I am to obey his wishes that means your father has no more than a few hours, a day or so at the most.'

The tears were running down Syrah's cheeks. She wiped them away with her fingertips but felt somehow more composed. She looked towards the four-poster bed and asked the doctor, 'Is there a problem about granting my father's last wishes?'

'No, not unless you or Caleb make one.'

'Then Ethan must die as he wanted to, with dignity and in this room as he has always known it. I'm certain Caleb will agree. Please make my father as comfortable as possible but have all these machines removed. Immediately! I need half an hour and then I'm moving in here to remain with my father. I know that's what he would want me to do.'

'My dear girl, I have no doubt about that nor that all your father was hanging on for was you. He'll drift away when he knows you are ready to let him go.'

'The mere sight of Ethan, feeling his hand in mine has given me strength. It's restored my confidence to do what is right for him. I can think of nothing else. I don't want to think of anything else. I love my father so very much it's impossible for me to let him or myself down in his time of need. My time of intolerable loss. I intend to turn this final journey he is about to take into as beautiful and easy a passage as I can for him. He deserves nothing less.'

* * *

Syrah took a hurried bath and changed into a pair of wide silver grey linen trousers and a white silk crêpe-de-chine blouse. After that she went directly to the rooms Diana and Keoki had been given.

She placed an arm around her son, kissed him and took Diana's hand in hers. 'I need you two to support me more than I have ever needed anyone in my life. The news isn't good. We're going to lose your Poppy, Keoki. I promise, when the time is right, you can see him and kiss him farewell. But that's all I can promise. Keoki, I'm going to spend all my time with Ethan. That means I'll have no time for you or anything else. Can you understand that and let Diana play mummy for me?'

Keoki, choked up with the pain of having to lose his grandfather, could hardly speak.

'Yes,' he managed at last.

'And forgive me for abandoning you at a time when I should be with you to comfort you?'

He just managed a nod of his head. Mother and son kissed and hugged each other then. Tears were brimming in Diana's eyes when the two women briefly embraced and Syrah fled from the room.

She could hear Paula chiding Caleb about something. Seeing them at the foot of the stairs, she descended and asked, 'Can I have a quick word?'

Caleb, looking as if he welcomed the interruption, said, 'Yes, of course,' and the three of them went into the sitting room. For a brief moment Syrah saw a certain vulnerability in him that reminded her of the Caleb she had known before Paula, a kindly brother with a more generous heart.

She went straight to the point. 'I hope you agree with me that Dad should die as he wants to, with dignity?'

'Yes, certainly,' answered Caleb.

'I'm moving into his room, to stay with him and make him as comfortable as I can.'

'I rather expected you would,' said Paula. And for once there was no facetiousness in her voice. She was too relieved that Syrah had taken over a role she herself did not want to play.

Syrah left the sitting room and a silent Caleb and Paula. In the hall she met Mr Wang who accompanied her to Ethan's room where they found him still with his eyes closed. Under the doctor's instructions the nurses were disengaging the last of the medical equipment, rolling and carrying what seemed like an inordinate amount of hospital machinery from the room. All that remained were oxygen tanks and a nurse's station: a table containing all they might need to keep their patient comfortable hidden by a sixteenth-century tapestry screen.

A more comfortable chair replaced the one alongside the bed. Mr Wang set a marble-topped Directoire table next to that and on it a silver tray with a cut glass decanter of malt whisky, a glass tumbler and a plate of smoked salmon sandwiches that he had carried into the room.

By the time Syrah sat in the chair, placed now so that she could hold her father's hand and they could look at each other, Ethan was free of any visible medical wiring except for a slim line of oxygen. He was dressed in the top half of a pair of coral-coloured silk pyjamas: Chinese dragons woven into the fine silk showed faintly in the soft warm light of a lamp standing on the table next to the bed.

Syrah leaned forward and rearranged the collar. The silk felt soft and luxurious. She ran her hand down the sleeve and adjusted the cuff. Memories flooded back as she took his hand in hers and stroked it.

'That Christmas so many years ago . . . we always called it "The Christmas of the silk pyjamas." I bought them on that bi-plane exhibition and display I attended in Hong Kong. You still look handsome in them. Remember what you said on first seeing them? "Syrah, they're fit for an Emperor. Every man at some time in his life would like at least once to feel like a royal, if only in bed. What a grand present." You're wearing them now, Ethan.'

As she turned away from her father to speak to Mr Wang, she felt a faint squeeze of her hand and turned back to see her father open his eyes and blink at her.

'You understood every word I said! Oh, thank God.'

Ethan blinked several times more and squeezed her hand again. Was there more strength in his grasp? Did she imagine it? Did she imagine renewed light in his eyes? Nurse Crumb was approaching the bed but Syrah waved her back.

'We'll beat this, Ethan.'

She read his lips as he formed them into a definite,

'No.' It took time and tremendous effort before quite clearly, in a whisper, he added, 'Love you, Syrah.'

She turned to Mr Wang and the three nurses standing near the window, watching their patient and his daughter. The look of astonishment on their faces was proof enough to her that her father was rallying. She knew in her heart that it was not to be for long and that was not because the doctor and nurses had told her so but because her father had. Ethan had never lied to her.

She smiled at the others in the room. An hour, several, a day or days, no matter how little or how much time Ethan had left on this earth, she intended to spend it with him, as pleasantly and peacefully as she could make it for them both. He knew he was going to die and was not frightened at the prospect. Ethan was living now to make certain Syrah need not fear for him and his passing. He and his daughter had always been able to read each other's feelings; they had been that close ever since she was a child.

Still holding his hand, she called the nurses over to her. At that moment the doctor returned to the room and went directly to Ethan. Everyone in the room, including Caleb and Paula who had followed in the doctor's footsteps, heard Ethan say in an exhausted whisper, 'Thank you, Abe, my children.'

It was not difficult to understand that he was thanking them for obeying his instructions on how he wished to end his life. No one seemed to know what to say next and it fell to Syrah to break the silence. She spoke first to

Mr Wang. 'Ethan loves flowers, especially white ones in this room, masses of Casablanca lilies in that Ming vase on the table over there, and white roses, three dozen, in the vase he usually has on the library table.'

She turned to gaze into her father's eyes and told him, 'I always thought it was so clever of you to turn that turret at the end of the room into a library. I remember even as a child adoring the adventure of walking up those winding stone stairs surrounded by book-lined walls.'

'You can draw from the flowers Dad has received from well wishers, Mr Wang,' suggested Paula.

'As long as they are what my father likes,' added Syrah.

'I think we're too many here, Dad. We don't want to tire you out. Paula and I will leave you with Syrah.' Then turning to his sister, Caleb suggested, 'We'll talk later about a roster.'

No, we won't, Caleb! was what went through her mind. But she said nothing. He was, after all, trying to do his best for all concerned: he could not help the coldness in his voice, the attempt to deal with these last hours of his father's life as if he were organising a work program. That was just Caleb.

Instead Syrah turned her attention to the nurses. 'I know how hard you've worked to save my father and the care you're giving him, but while I am grateful beyond words for what you are doing for him, I would ask you one further favour. Could you tend to him out of uniform, wearing dresses? Something bright to remind him of pretty women walking about in everyday life. It would be so nice for him if things appeared as normal as possible.'

Syrah felt Ethan squeeze her hand. She did know what he wanted!

Chapter 3

Syrah woke with a start. She very nearly leaped out of the chair, would have but for the blanket that had been tucked around her. Her first thought was for her father. She looked over her shoulder towards the four-poster bed. It was all right, he was still with them. She knew that because Miss Sanchez was sitting on a chair next to the bed, holding his hand.

Syrah relaxed with a deep sigh of relief. Who had covered her with the cashmere blanket, moved her chair and all to the window? When had she dozed off? She could remember nothing except that she had been talking to Ethan, who had seemed less anxious, more relaxed by the sound of her voice, but she couldn't remember what they were talking about. Yes, *they*, because he had managed an occasional word. It had been horribly difficult for him to speak but they had been conversing with each other in a fashion, she doing most of the talking. She was angry with herself. How could she have done that, just dropped off to sleep when he needed her? The whisky, the damned whisky! How stupid she had been to drink it.

She gazed out of the window at the sweeping view of row upon row of vines, green with leaves and heavy with fruit, climbing up the slopes facing the sun. There was movement going on: several pick-up trucks bumping along the unpaved tracks, people walking among the vines. Life was going on out there on the other side of the window pane. She had forgotten that life, normal living, was carrying on outside this room where everything had stopped for her and her father, mired by the coming of death and her distress.

She rose from the chair and went to her father. His eyes were closed. 'He's sleeping, he's had a comfortable night,' whispered Miss Sanchez.

Mrs Crumb approached Syrah from the nurse's station behind the screen and drew her aside, suggesting, 'We need to tend to your father, bathe him, change his sheets, make him comfortable. Why don't you take the time to bathe yourself and have breakfast and then come back? Let's say in an hour's time.'

'If there's a change . . .'

Mrs Crumb interrupted, 'I will come for you at once, I promise.'

'Please, you mustn't let me fall asleep again. I lost those precious hours of being with him. Who moved me? You should have just woken me up.'

'Your father wasn't alone. After your brother and I carried you over to the window, he sat with your father for a while and then Miss Sanchez took over. Now, you hurry along and we'll do what we must as fast as we can.'

Ethan was awake when Syrah returned. Incredibly he looked better and very handsome. She went directly to him and kissed him on the cheek and then the lips. He managed a slight smile or else she imagined it. For the first time it was he who managed to move his hand in an attempt to take hers. She grasped it and sat down.

'For a man in your state, Ethan, you look marvellous,' she told him.

'A dying man,' he told her in a slow and laboured drawl.

'Always insistent that I face the truth, no matter how bad it is – and you're still at it. You've always been that way with me: not wanting me to be afraid of the truth or the reality of what is. Accept it and get on with the life you want for yourself, that's what you taught me. I won't fail you, especially not in this the most terrible time of my life. Even now you're thinking of me, trying to help me to get over my fear and sadness. I won't say loss because I'll never lose you, I'll carry you in my heart always.'

Ethan squeezed her hand.

'Ah, you're telling me, "Right on". And you want no tears but for Caleb and me to celebrate your life in the mourning of your death.' And now Ethan squeezed her hand twice more.

A yes! Armed with the knowledge that she knew what her father wanted from her, Syrah asked herself, What do you do for someone you love who is dying? Just what we are doing: making his final journey from one world to another as pleasant and as easy as possible. Granting him his last wishes, surrounding him with love and all things beautiful. Not bothering him with my pain but putting that aside, removing all the burdens of life and living from him, setting him free so that he may use all his energies to rise above life and follow the light.

There was a knock at the door. Miss Sanchez opened it and stepped aside. Mr Wang entered the room followed by Caleb and Paula carrying vases of flowers, exactly the ones Syrah had ordered. The room was immediately transformed and the scent was sweet. Instinctively she knew she was doing everything right. On first arriving at her father's bedside she had walked into an alien place that had nothing to do with Ethan. What she had seen was a place of hospital technology, a room that had the stench of death about it. No more!

It now looked a more beautiful and hospitable place, brightened by his nurses in their pretty patterned dresses. A window had been opened and a soft warm breeze with the scent of the earth and growing vines on it wafted faintly into the room.

While Caleb and Paula stood around the bed, Syrah busied herself in the library, moving the vase from the table there in the hope that Ethan might see flowers in it by his bed. Rubenstein playing Chopin was the music she chose for his room; she ignored the look of disapproval on Paula's face and adjusted the volume. It was lower but most definitely there. Caleb and Paula did not stay long. They most cordially suggested to Syrah that she send word when she wanted them to release her from her vigil.

Paula looking round the room from the doorway could not resist a final barb. 'Syrah – always the partygirl. One would think you were getting ready to receive guests here.'

'Sadly I'm not, Paula. But it's a great compliment to my father that it looks that way. You see, I'm only interpreting his wishes.' And she walked to take her seat by his side.

'It's one of those late-summer days, Ethan, the kind you love so much. The sun on the vines is really warm. What happy times we've had together on days like this! You've always given me so much, never failed me. Even now I can remember running through the rows of vines as a child. How you took pains to teach me about the grapes and wine, how to cut and trim the vines, harvest alongside the pickers. Those marvellous long tables of food and drink for the workers. I was always so proud to sit down with them and you to eat and drink.

'It was so easy to adore you, first as a father and then when I was older as a man and a friend. I've always respected you for your accomplishments, the love you've had for the vineyard and the pride you take in your wine. Those high and low points in my life . . . you saw me through them, shared them with me, made certain that I never had to face them alone. Thank you, thank you for all of that.'

Ethan raised her hand ever so slowly and placed it

briefly to his lips. Then he told her, 'I always loved your spirit. When you love something it's easy to be there for it. I saw myself in you.'

That much talking seemed to exhaust him. He closed his eyes and squeezed her hand. She was learning to understand his signals, this new form of communication between them. The closing of the eyes meant, Time to rest, over to you. The pressure on her hand meant, Yes, or, I love you, or, That's right, what I want.

She had had her own pattern of communication going with Ethan: holding his hand and stroking it so as to let him know the warmth of life and love, a reminder that it was still there for him; her endless stream of a nearly one-sided conversation to keep him alert and comforted by the sound of her voice. Syrah and her father had always shown their affection for each other not in words but in deeds. She was therefore deeply affected by his struggle to express his feeling for her in words so she might remember them always and forever.

Suddenly she saw more clearly those years of pure joy she had lived as a child and an adolescent when she ran free and grew up in the vineyards. Syrah realised not only how much she loved her father but Richebourg-Conti too. It had occurred to her only briefly on the flight here that when Ethan was gone from her life so would the vineyard be, her family home, and even the income she derived from it. That thought returned. She felt sick. It was all too terrifying to contemplate. Like a drowning woman, her own life flashed before her.

When she had turned twenty, Syrah had carved a fast life in a bigger, wider world than the Valley afforded her. She had the looks, temperament, intelligence, and an adventurous spirit, a great passion to live. Her father had not been disapproving of how she wanted to live, more disappointed that her love for Richebourg-Conti was not enough to keep her there to work with him in the wine industry. Ethan therefore had given her the option: her share of the vineyard in monetary terms to fund the fast life she hungered for, but with the understanding that on Ethan's death, Caleb alone would inherit Richebourg-Conti. Syrah had made her decision: money over work. She had no regrets, was making no excuses for the choice she had made, but did reflect that youth rarely thinks about legacy above its own lust for life.

She felt the slightest pressure on her hand: Ethan signalling that he wanted her to talk to him. She stroked his hand and told him, 'It has quite suddenly hit me how much I love Richebourg-Conti. Oh, over the years I sometimes yearned, but always briefly, to be more a part of the Valley, closer to the earth, this place where I was born, but it never occurred to me that I love Richebourg-Conti in the same passionate way that you do. Not until now.'

Syrah felt a very light pressure on her hand and looked at her father. Ethan opened his eyes. Father and daughter gazed at each other.

'You knew! You have always known, that's what you're telling me!' she said, astonished.

'Yes, banked on it,' he answered.

Syrah could see what an effort it was for him to speak those few words. She was terribly moved that he should know her better than she knew herself. That even now, in his last hours of life, he could manage to let her know that her realisation of how much Richebourg-Conti meant to her pleased him, was important to him. It moved her deeply, so much so that she felt compelled to turn her face away from him for a few minutes so that she might compose herself and not show that she was near to tears.

She rose from the chair, telling him, 'Don't exhaust yourself, Ethan, let me do the talking.'

He closed his eyes and Syrah kissed his hand and placed it on the coverlet. 'I'm going to leave you just long enough to put on another CD. That lovely ethereal music of Rameau you love so much. French court music, why not?'

While searching for the CD, Syrah pondered on what she had just said to him. It was true, she did love Richebourg-Conti in the same way he did – very differently from the way Caleb and Paula felt about it. They had always been blatant about their lust for power, money, prestige. For more than a decade she had known they viewed Richebourg-Conti as a vehicle they could use to diversify and build their own empire upon. But always Ethan had been there to thwart such schemes. With him gone, who would there be to curb their ambition? For the first time Syrah felt tremendous anxiety at the idea she would never be a part of Richebourg-Conti again.

To lose father and heritage at the same time – she wondered how she was going to cope with this double blow.

When she returned to sit at her father's side and take his hand in hers, she could not be sure but thought she saw a more relaxed expression on his face. It held a certain contentment that had always been a part of Ethan before he'd had this terrible stroke.

She sensed he was drifting away from her, leaving behind the world and his children, his wine and his beloved vines, and he was all right about it. How cruel it would be when he was already so far on his final journey to try and pull him back in order to persuade him to change his will, make her an equal shareholder in the vineyard and winery so that she could become a part of Richebourg-Conti, protect it as he had during his entire working life. It was asking too much too late of a man who was way past dealing with worldly affairs: a wayward daughter, a greedy, weak son and an ambitious daughter-in-law.

Instead she chose to read to him from a first edition of Proust's *Remembrance Of Things Past*, one of several books on the table next to his bed. The book fell open where he had placed a marker. Syrah removed it and began to read aloud. When Miss Turtle approached her to whisper that she would relieve her, Syrah politely refused the offer and continued reading.

The nurse checked her patient's pulse then reported to Miss Crumb that she could not find one. From the library Mrs Crumb made a discreet call to the doctor.

Paula, Caleb and their children made a brief visit. Syrah acknowledged them with a nod of the head but continued reading. She somehow felt she mustn't stop. Nor did she when a few minutes later Diana brought Keoki in. He kissed his mother on the cheek, she smiled at him and the boy went round the other side of the bed with Diana. First she kissed Ethan on the cheek and then Keoki kissed his grandfather.

When they closed Ethan's bedroom door behind them, Keoki remarked to Diana, 'I wasn't frightened at all. The music and Mama reading, Grandfather dozing so peacefully . . . do you think he felt my kiss? I hope so. If it's true what Aunt Paula has told us, that he'll be leaving us soon, I'd like him to have my kiss to take with him.'

Several hours later brought a glorious sunset, one that turned the room into a soft golden colour. It was then that the doctor finally arrived. Flanked by the nurses he went directly to his patient and, after examining him, round the bedside to Syrah who never looked up from her book or stopped reading. The doctor removed the book from her hand and closed it. At last Syrah fell silent. Then he unwound her fingers from Ethan's hand. She had never let it go, not even when hours before she had sensed there was no life left in it. She placed a hand over her mouth to stop herself from screaming and gazed at her father for the first time since she had opened the book.

Syrah felt an uncomfortable tightness in her chest, a pounding in her head and her heart. Tears poured down her cheeks for several minutes. She took several deep breaths and regained her composure. Only then did she allow the doctor and Miss Turtle to help her from her chair.

It was late afternoon the following day when Syrah awakened. Mr Wang brought her breakfast in bed: blueberry pancakes, sausages, scrambled eggs and a pot of hot black coffee. It surprised Syrah and Mr Wang how ravenous she was.

'Are you all right? Is there anything I can do for you, Miss Syrah?' asked the old retainer.

She answered, 'Nothing will ever be the same for either of us, Mr Wang. I think we will both be lonely for my father forever. Are you all right?'

She seemed to Mr Wang to be coping but sadness and distress were plain on her face and the trembling of her hands. He answered that he was.

While eating her breakfast she did not think about Ethan but the fragility of life. How it can so quickly be snuffed out, changing in a moment as hers had. Overnight she'd lost her father, her greatest ally, the most important man in her life, for certain her income and her financial security, even Richebourg-Conti, for wouldn't Caleb and Paula see to that? An overwhelming sense of isolation from all she had ever loved and felt kinship to, with the exception of her son and Diana, washed over her. She felt adrift and alone in the world without a rudder. It was all too much to take in, too frightening even to think about.

Mr Wang sat with Syrah, watching her eat as he had

done numerous times since she was a child. He had always been a friend to her as well as Ethan's devoted Man Friday. He left only when Diana arrived with Keoki who immediately climbed into bed with his mother, to kiss her and eat off her plate.

For the five days before the funeral Syrah, Keoki and Diana had Château Richebourg-Conti more or less to themselves. Caleb and Paula arrived several times to share a meal with them and to discuss details of the funeral. They never brought their children to play with Keoki, never extended an invitation for the trio to dine at their house. Syrah was grateful for how civil they were being but was disturbed by how cordial rather than friendly they were. Still it was better than the indifference Caleb and Paula usually showed her when she returned for a visit. Was it possible Ethan's death would bring them closer together?

Keoki, Diana and Syrah spent their time together touring the vineyards, cellars, winery, and talking to the many workers. They were making an effort but sadness was unavoidable. The three of them talked about Ethan, told stories to each other about him and the good times they had had, stories that reflected his charm and zest for life. He was still very much alive for them.

They received the odd visitor paying a condolence call and then one day James Whitehawk appeared. Syrah saw him walk through the front door into the hall and greet Mr Wang. The two men, who had known each other all James's life, exchanged bear hugs. Sadness showed clearly in James's eyes as he looked over Mr Wang's shoulder and up the stairs where Syrah stood. He stepped away from Mr Wang and without a word Syrah walked down the stairs and into his arms. They kissed and James stroked her hair then they kissed again, an open and passionate kiss that warmed Syrah's heart and stirred sensuous sensations. She knew at once that here he was, the man who could love her as she needed to be loved. And she had always loved him, only until now she had never known how much. Was it possible that until a few days ago she had never been receptive enough to accept such intense feelings of love as he had always felt for her?

Syrah was overwhelmed with gratitude that he should return to her in her most dire moment of need. Her first love, the one she had left behind so very long ago. It quite shocked and yet thrilled her that he was here for her now. She felt a surge of life that she'd thought never to experience again. She'd feared it had been snuffed out with the last breath her father had taken.

James released her. Still holding her hands, he said, 'I was away in Seattle – I came as soon as I heard. Just remember, I'm here for you.'

'You always have been.'

James looked embarrassed as he answered, 'Yes.'

Together they walked into what had been Ethan's study. She could feel his sadness, deep and consuming. He had loved Ethan all his life, was near to tears now.

'Ethan loved you, James. He was there the day you

were born. Remember how he used to tell us about it when we were children? You and your family and your vineyard were not just our next-door neighbours – he took pride in being close to you all and to Whitehawk Ridge. He was so delighted when you received your doctorate degree and returned to Whitehawk Ridge to work the vineyard. And what about that party he gave for you! What fun we all had. He often talked to me about you and your feeling for wine. He said you genuinely loved the land and had an innate knowledge of how to get the best from it, just as your father did. Oh, yes, Ethan loved you.'

'Syrah, what can I say? What can I do?'

'Just what you are doing, be here for me.'

Choked with emotion, confused by the intense erotic attraction surfacing between them at a time when they'd least expected it, they fell silent. They felt the vital presence of Ethan still lingering in his room and let it envelop them. Syrah sensed warmth and love, and her mind wandered back to the days when James and she were children and inseparable.

She thought then of James's father, Inabe Whitehawk, Ethan's great friend, and how their fathers used to take her and James on excursions: to wine tastings or visiting the small growers for luncheon parties. She thought now of the innumerable times Ethan and she would walk from Ruy Blas, the smallest of the Richebourg-Conti vineyards that bordered on to Inabe Whitehawk's vineyard, Whitehawk Ridge, to share a bottle of wine and snack on deep fried American Indian delicacies for which James's mother was famous.

Syrah tried to remember why she and James had drifted apart. One day they were inseparable and the next just good friends, then acquaintances. She had always put it down to growing up. How had it all gone so wrong for them? The idea that love and commitment could have meant so little to her was too much to think about now. She needed some time, some space. She rose from the settee where they were sitting.

Standing next to her, James sensed it was appropriate for him to leave. They had overwhelmed each other with feelings they'd thought would never happen for them again.

Ethan Richebourg's funeral was attended by many people from all walks of life: friends, relatives, associates from the wine world who had come from several continents to pay their last respects to a man who had been a legend. The church was filled to capacity.

The graveside service completed, coffin resting under a covering woven of lily-of-the-valley, people already dispersing to the cars that would take them back to Richebourg-Conti – the funeral ordeal was nearly over.

Caleb looked around at the many major and respected players at the high end of the wine trade who had given him their condolences with a new esteem now that Ethan had passed the mantle to his son. He considered the many beautiful women who, since Ethan had been widowed, had been a part of his father's life and was astonished at the genuine grief that showed in their faces. His gaze fell on his sister. Syrah was looking beautiful even in her grief. She was standing proud with her half-breed son, her friend Diana behind her. He saw her as he imagined everyone did, the prodigal daughter returned. The bitter taste of resentment lingered in his mouth. His new sense of power goaded him on like a spur in his flesh.

He kept his anger under control until he, Paula and Syrah were alone and walking away from the grave towards the waiting limousine.

'Well, it's almost over. The reception at the house and the reading of the will, then there'll be only the loss of a father to deal with. I dare say that's going to be more difficult for you, Syrah, than for me. You were, after all, closer to Father than I was. He saw to that with his blatant favouritism which you ruthlessly took advantage of. Have you any idea how painful that always was for Paula and me? How embarrassing? Never once did you work at earning the love he lavished on you as Paula and I have done. *And*, I might add, to no avail! I can never remember you, who had so much influence over him, even once interceding for us with Father for something *we* wanted, something that might have changed our lives, delivered us from his autocratic rule.'

Paula slipped her arm through her husband's and told him, 'That's all over, Caleb. Ethan's gone and you and I are in control now. There's no need to upset yourself anymore about sibling rivalry, the unfairness of favouritism. It's coloured our lives long enough.'

And to Syrah she added, 'It's true, you know, we've inherited everything. Ethan told us that years ago when you came of age and chose to take your share of the estate to finance your self-indulgent high life. The reading of the will this afternoon will make it official. That's why you must be there to hear it and know we did not cheat you out of anything. You cheated yourself.'

Syrah, sunk deeply into her sorrow, felt every word like the sting of a whip on her bare flesh. There was nothing for her to do but rise above the pain. Puzzled by their insensitivity, she pointed out, 'Father isn't even in the ground yet, why are you talking about control of Richebourg-Conti?'

'Because above or below the ground, Ethan is dead and has been for nearly a week. So I suggest, maybe for the first time in your life, you start thinking how *you* will support yourself and Keoki without him and Richebourg-Conti bankrolling your lifestyle.'

'Paula, I can't think about myself right now, never mind five minutes into the future. But rest assured, whatever my circumstances I will not impose myself or my needs on you and Caleb.'

'I'm relieved to hear that,' said her sister-in-law, who did indeed look relieved.

'You astound me, Paula, you and my brother. The hostility you have for me, the bitterness. What have I ever done to warrant such extreme dislike? The love of a father for a daughter? That's pathetic. That I lived my life as I wanted to? Well, so did you and I don't hate you for that. You now have Richebourg-Conti, control of one of the premier vineyards in the world, to do with as you please. You have all you have ever wanted, and still you feel nothing but anger and contempt for me. Why?'

Years of pent-up anger against Syrah prompted Paula to blurt out, 'Because when you were living the life you wanted to live, it was at great cost to me and my family. What we wanted to make of our lives. A once-in-a-lifetime opportunity came Caleb's way. It was a chance for your brother and me to go independent and strike out on our own, get out from under Ethan's control of Richebourg-Conti and working for him like lackeys for *his* vineyards, *his* wine.

'More than ten years ago our neighbour, the Bandellero Creek vineyard and winery, badly neglected and in need of modernisation, was offered to Caleb. It had the potential to become another Richebourg-Conti and we wanted to take it on. Ethan refused to lend us the half a million dollars we needed to buy it – and all because of *you* and your irresponsible, frivolous lifestyle! You were living the high life, choosing a handsome gigolo for sex and surfing, and Ethan had to buy off your Hawaiian lover so you could gain sole custody of your half-caste bastard. He refused us because of *you* and Richebourg-Conti's contractual obligation to pay you your share of the business. Oh, there was always *money* for Syrah, never for us.'

'Paula!' There was a note of anger in Caleb's voice.

'Your brother thinks I've gone too far. Don't be a hypocrite, Caleb. You bear the same grudge as I do against Syrah. Admit it. Had she not systematically drained the coffers of Richebourg-Conti, allowed to by Ethan, we would have had Bandellero Creek and a whole different life,' she chided her husband.

Caleb pulled her away by the arm and marched her to the waiting limousine. Husband and wife didn't say another word to each other then. Paula's eyes were brimming with tears, anger and bitterness plain on her face. He helped her into the car and closed the door on her.

'Where are you going, Caleb?' she asked finally.

'To get Syrah. She's riding back to the house with us, in case you've forgotten? And though all you said was true, I don't want to hear another word. This is neither the time nor the place.'

'Oh, my God! You're going soft on her. You vowed to me that when Richebourg-Conti was ours, she would be off the land and out of our lives. Well, you'd better make sure that's exactly what happens.'

With Paula's tirade still ringing in his ears, Caleb slammed the car door and walked towards Syrah who had not moved from where he had left her. His wife's outburst was a reminder to him of the years of bickering between them, vis-à-vis the loss of Bandellero Creek, money for Syrah, how Ethan had favoured her rather than Caleb, Paula and their children. It had hardened his wife, caused many breaches in their marriage. Had she, after all, wanted so much? To have a winery of their own out from under the Richebourg-Conti umbrella. For Ethan to set Syrah aside, just once, in favour of his son. Ethan had been wrong not to lend them the money, to ruin Caleb's and Paula's chances of leaving Richebourg-Conti in favour of their own enterprise.

The wealth and power that he and Paula had in and out of the wine world, the life they led as heirs apparent to Richebourg-Conti, were compensations in part but never quite made up for losing their chance to create a marvellous label of their own, on their own, without Ethan. One that they could proudly have added to Richebourg-Conti once Caleb did inherit. That would have made them the premier vineyard and winery in the Valley. He was painfully aware that frustrated ambition and sibling rivalry had undermined his life. Such hatred in the soul did not die easily.

Chapter 4

On the ride back to the château, Syrah remained shocked by the degree of dislike her brother and sister-in-law had showed for her. It was true: She was spoiled, pampered, and had been loved by her father and many people, liked by even more. All her life she had danced to the tune of laughter, fun and adventure; played with love. She was devoid of guile and because she lacked any understanding of hatred and treachery, recognition of it in Caleb and Paula had been a long time coming. Now that she had been made to see them clearly, she hardly knew how to cope. All she wanted was to run away.

As she stepped from the limousine and saw the terraces and reception rooms of Château Richebourg-Conti, filled with people there to pay their last respects to her father, her strength returned. With every handshake and kind word for him, every warm kiss on her cheek from someone who had known what he stood for as a man, a father and a friend, she was able to lift herself above the shock Caleb and Paula had dealt her.

So many years away from the Valley and still friends

and neighbours she had grown up with and left behind in her rage to live were there for her and behaving towards her as if she had never left. Syrah was moved by seeing them again. They mingled easily with her other friends and the aristocracy of the wine world who'd arrived from the far corners of the earth. Suddenly she was aware that this was her world too, a place where she belonged as Ethan had.

Looking across the room over a sea of people, Syrah and James's eyes found each other. She was incredibly pleased to see him. They smiled and she started to make her way towards him.

James was standing among a group of other small vineyard owners. Like James and Ethan these were men dedicated to their vineyards and the production of fine wine. Each of them had spent a lifetime trying to raise the standard of their wine to compete with Richebourg-Conti's premier label, Ruy Blas. This had been Ethan's pride and joy. It had brought him world-wide recognition and prizes galore. Richebourg-Conti's Ruy Blas made Master of Wine Ethan Richebourg a legendary name in the high end of the wine market.

The men had been telling stories of how during bad times, as they were having now, Ethan had come to their rescue. How they had on occasion sided with him to save their valley from the predators who stalked it, not to produce wine but to grab land for commercial development. Not a man in the group believed they would have the support of Richebourg-Conti now that Caleb and Paula were in charge. They had in the past given the small growers good reason for thinking otherwise, notably their association with Ira Rudman who was ambitious where Napa Valley property and the smaller, more troubled vineyards were involved.

James was still looking across the room at Syrah, standing with a boy he presumed was her son, when one of the group he was with, said, 'If the daughter had only inherited then we would have had a friend at Richebourg-Conti.'

Syrah's heart lifted when on seeing James across the room she felt once again that sensual attraction, love emanating from him to her as their eyes met. She wanted to run into his arms. But this was happening too fast, at the wrong time and in the wrong place, she told herself. She distracted her feelings for him by placing an arm around Keoki and kissing the top of his head. She managed a faint smile for Diana who was trying to disengage herself from her admiring public.

Syrah marvelled at the way her friend always attracted a crowd of men and women around her. She was one of those rare screen goddesses who had about them an air of serene innocence and self-sufficiency. A fine actress before the cameras and on the stage, she never played the role of movie star for her own enjoyment. It was part of her charm, why her public loved her. She always made the man in the street feel she was approachable. Finally she was able to join Syrah and her godson.

'Go downstairs to the kitchen, Keo. Cook has a meal prepared for you,' Syrah told the boy.

'I'm not hungry. I'll wait until later and eat with you and Diana.'

'No. Now, Keo. It will be hours before we do something about food. Please, make an effort. You've eaten nothing all day and precious little last night. We have to get past this, Keo.'

Mother and son knew what she meant and the boy reluctantly went below stairs. Several people stopped to say goodbye to her before she had a chance to take Diana aside and tell her that she should be ready to leave Richebourg-Conti before five o'clock when the will was due to be read in the library.

'Is that wise?' asked Diana, always the practical one.

'And hear another tirade of abuse such as I just had to listen to at the graveside? I'll not attend the reading of the will and give them the satisfaction of hearing they're sole owners of Richebourg-Conti. They'll only say something more to humiliate me, and do I need that?'

'Listen, for as long as I've known you, you've always managed to sidestep their barbs. Ignore them like you always have and attend the reading of the will. Richebourg-Conti is theirs and you've always known that's the way it was going to be. But Ethan would have wanted you to be there, Syrah. He loved Keoki and might have left him something to be remembered by.'

'In his lifetime Ethan was always generous to Keoki with money and his personal possessions, things he wanted the boy and no one else to have. He was wise, knew how Paula and Caleb felt about having a half-caste bastard for a nephew. That they would give nothing to Keoki, will or no will. Ethan wanted there to be no problem about Keoki receiving the things so he handled that while he was alive. So no, Diana, there'll be nothing in the will for Keoki and I'll not watch Paula gloat over that!'

'Instinct tells me you should be there for the reading, Syrah.'

'I'll think about it,' she answered despondently.

'Good,' announced Diana.

'What's good?'

The two women turned around and came face to face with Ira Rudman. He said all the things everyone says at such a time. Diego Juarez was with him. He placed one arm around Syrah and kissed her. Diego had been to the church service and to the cemetery; it had been he who had offered the blanket of lily-of-the-valley for Ethan's coffin. It was similar to the one he had chosen for his own father's funeral.

Syrah knew how sad Diego was about Ethan's death but Ira . . . Ethan and he had not been close, Ethan having disliked several schemes Ira had approached Richebourg-Conti with through Caleb and Paula. So what was he doing there at all? she asked herself. She had not invited him to the cemetery or to the house, which had been by invitation only. She was certain Diana hadn't been in contact with him either. But whatever one thought of Ira, he was not socially crass or pushy, he knew his manners. Caleb and Paula must have asked him. All that was going through her mind as they stood around drinking champagne and eating canapés off the many silver trays being passed around the room by family, staff and helpers.

Syrah excused herself to walk through the crowd towards James, drawn to him once again by his handsome looks, serenity, and at the same time the sensual promise that lingered in his eyes and around his mouth. His spirit she had always known to be honest and kind. His incredible strength as a human being, his passion for life, love and the earth, seemed to be reaching out to her now as they had never done before.

She thought of those times in the last ten years when she had seen him from a distance to wave to or to blow a kiss. Or briefly, close up, merely to say hello. At those times she had looked admiringly at his marvellous face: the high cheekbones, long straight nose, sexy lips and black, almond-shaped eyes that were slightly hooded. On those occasions James had usually been wearing jeans and a white shirt, and always his leather belt with an antique Navaho buckle adorned with a large chunk of turquoise. Once she had seen him in a leather jacket. She thought he looked so different now: smart and sophisticated in an Armani suit, and possibly even more sexy.

He was a full-blooded Native American of the Yurok tribe and the smoothness of his tawny-coloured skin and straight jet black hair worn to just above the collar of his jacket, the long, muscular body, had always been sensually interesting to Syrah in those brief moments when they had seen each other. But she had been too busy with her Malibu life to do anything about it. In the midst of her sadness and the family strife she was distracted by the thought that leaving James Whitehawk behind when she left the Valley might just have been a mistake.

She joined a group of men whom she did not know and offered her hands to James. He took them in his and held them while telling her, 'Syrah, this is a sad day for us all. My deepest sympathy, I know what Ethan meant to you.'

He made lengthy introductions, explaining to Syrah as he went along who the men were and what vineyards they owned.

James and Syrah were cautious with one another, both sensing they wanted to know more about each other, where they were in their lives. *She* knew only the most rudimentary facts about him: that he was married, the father of two girls whom he adored, his vineyard small but prestigious. *He* knew that she was a single mother of a boy whose father was Hawaiian, and that she lived a jet-set lifestyle and flew her own plane. No more, in short, than anyone in the wine trade already knew.

In spite of working at playing down their attraction for one another, for a brief moment sexual sparks flew between them and something happened. Embarrassed by their feelings they broke the momentary spell when James reached out to a man passing by and took his arm, wanting Syrah to meet him. He continued introducing her to people there whom she had never met: small, struggling, not so successful growers, the less famous wine people of the Valley who nevertheless saw Ethan's death as a great personal loss.

They had grown to quite a good-sized group before Syrah realised that they were her father's kind of people: passionate about their industry and the betterment of it. Then a man she had seen before joined them.

James introduced Syrah to Sam Holbrook, owner of a cooperage famous as one of the best on either side of the Atlantic. His name was familiar to Syrah as a long-time business acquaintance and friend to Richebourg-Conti, and in particular Ethan. Her mind flashed back to her father who had often spoken to her of Sam. She imagined them together, vital and exciting men who enjoyed themselves in work and at play. And she thought, Oh, Ethan, such a blow to lose you for so many people.

It had been at the church, when Syrah had approached Caleb and Paula about the cars going to the cemetery, that she'd first seen Sam. The three of them were talking about the service. Neither her brother nor her sister-in-law bothered to introduce them. In spite of that, for a second their eyes had met and one of those inexplicable instant attractions happened that can flare between strangers. That look declared they knew they would meet again and be friends. And, thought Syrah, here we are.

It had been obvious to Sam that the lack of an

introduction had been deliberate, Paula and Caleb's freezing indifference towards Syrah had been blatant. It had long ago registered with him that Paula Richebourg was an over-ambitious, self-promoting bitch. Now, with Ethan gone, she was wasting no time in wielding her power, cutting Ethan's favourite down to size. It was remembering this incident that decided him to befriend Syrah. He sensed she would need every real friend she could get now her father was gone.

James and several other men shook hands with Sam, and James introduced him to Syrah.

'We should have met before,' he told her.

'Well, we have now.'

'Yes, and you must consider me your friend, for Ethan's sake. Remember you can always, at any time, call on me.' And he gallantly raised her hand to place a kiss upon it.

Syrah realised that Sam had picked up on the hostility that her brother and sister-in-law felt for her. She was relieved that someone had seen it, that it was not something she had over-reacted to when they'd expressed it so clearly at the cemetery.

The men were all talking wine and barrels, Sam being the supplier to most of them. Syrah listened but a wave of sadness overwhelmed her. Why Ethan? So fine and vital a human being, such an exciting and romantic figure in the wine world, why had he had to die and not be there among these men today, talking wine and barrels? And why couldn't Caleb and Paula continue his dreams, follow the path he wanted Richebourg-Conti to travel? She felt quite sick to think that there was every chance they might not do that.

She gazed around the room and saw Diana, looking beautiful and elegant in her black crêpe dress. Several men were standing around her, she was pouring champagne into their glasses. But it didn't look as if they were truly celebrating Ethan's life, which was what he would have liked, there was no joy in their faces. She saw Ira standing with Caleb and Paula and half a dozen other people. They looked very pleased with themselves, the cats who had swallowed the canary. There was something too smooth in the way they looked, both solicitous and scheming at the same time. Paula kept touching Ira's arm, on occasion gazing flirtatiously into his eyes. The room seemed to be dividing itself into two camps. In one the friends and colleagues of Ethan Richebourg; in the other friends and associates of Caleb and Paula, the new owners of Richebourg-Conti.

Syrah felt as if she had stepped out of her own skin and was watching herself, observing everything. Was this all a bad dream or was she sleepwalking? She didn't pinch herself, she didn't have to because though she felt she could be doing either she knew that what was happening was all too real. She was awake but moving around zombie-like, there but not there.

Unable to bear her sadness at losing so much of her life in one fell swoop – father, family, home, and all they have given her over the years – Syrah slipped unobtrusively away from the group to walk in the garden where she could be alone and collect her thoughts.

All the time she was walking through the house, down the stairs and into the garden, she kept telling herself she was letting herself and Ethan down. She should be able to rise above Caleb and Paula slapping her around emotionally. Enough was enough. It was as if something snapped in her head or Ethan whispered, 'my own true girl' in her ear. She was back and was herself. She had a life of her own to go back to in Malibu. She checked her watch. Not long before the reading of the will in the library. She was Syrah Richebourg and she belonged here. She could and would face Caleb and Paula's moment of triumph and walk away from them with great dignity after she had said her final piece.

A coral-coloured sun was still high in the bright blue sky. The silence of the garden had eased Syrah's pain. She walked through it and with every step seemed to gain emotional stability, so that for the first time since her father's death she was able to relive those last hours they'd had together and how much they had meant, would always mean, to her for the rest of her life. They had, in a fashion, said their farewells and she had sent Ethan off free from worry about her. They had done the best they could for each other in life and death.

James was practically upon her when she turned around to face him. Their many years of separation seemed to fall away and memories of what they had meant to each other as children growing up together – sweet and innocent first love, playing in the vineyards, riding and swimming together, sharing a lust for adventure and life – came flooding back. In an instant, when they gazed into each other's eyes, something more than special, quite extraordinary, happened to them. Without thought or hesitation Syrah stepped into his outstretched arms.

Wrapping himself around her, he held her tight until they could feel the warmth of each other's bodies. He stroked her hair and kissed her lips and brushed away the tears cascading down her cheeks. For several minutes they lost themselves in each other. The world, with all its goodness and badness, its joys and its tragedies, vanished for them.

He slipped his hands under the wide kimono sleeves of her black silk wraparound dress and caressed her arms; searched out her naked breasts and caressed them, felt the weight and the succulent roundness of them in his hands. His caress had nothing to do with lust, only comfort and caring. She gave in to the sensation and the last tears she would ever shed for her father dried. Clear-eyed now, new life and passion began to flow through her once more. Being in James's arms felt good, so very right. Only now did something more than carnal attraction come to light for them: the yearning to experience with each other sensual delight, wanting to come together in that special oneness they sensed was there for them. It was too marvellous and so for some time they just stood there in the garden enveloped in each other's arms, healing themselves from the wounds life had inflicted upon them through the many years they had been apart.

From the terrace Ira watched the scene being played out below in the garden until Syrah and James parted, spoke briefly and she walked swiftly away from him to break into a run towards the house.

Ira was seeing a very different Syrah. There was the unmistakable look of love in her eyes and he seethed with jealousy. He had not wooed her for so many years to lose her now. He could thrash her for even allowing the possibility that he might.

Diana, in the house, passed a window by chance and spotted Ira on the terrace below, watching Syrah. She saw him crunch an empty champagne flute in his hand. It splintered. He opened his hand and the shards fell on to the stones. There was a look of lust and anger on his face that told her everything. He wanted to be the man who held Syrah in his arms, for her to look at him as she had looked at that other man. Ira wanted Syrah! For how long had he lusted after her? Yet again she felt betrayed by Ira. Diana asked herself how she could possibly have missed the fact that the man she had loved so completely was infatuated with her best friend?

She came away from the window and leaned against a wall. It was inevitable that questions about Ira and Syrah should be running through her mind. Hadn't she always suspected that Syrah held a sexual attraction for Ira but blanked that possibility out of her mind? She had, over the years, learned to look and not see so many things in order to stay with him.

Feeling even a residue of love for such a cad was excruciatingly painful for her. Especially since Ira claimed he still wanted her in his life. He insisted all Diana had to come to terms with was what they were and were not to each other, adjust to it, and then they could live happily ever after. If there had been even the slightest chance she would give in to his wishes, this final betrayal had killed it. Her love for Ira was quite dead.

On entering the house, Syrah was immediately caught up saying goodbye to several people who were leaving and tried to put all thoughts of James and what had happened in the garden out of her mind. How at a sad time like this could such a thing as falling in love happen to her? It was a kind of madness that she should love James, feel a passion for him she had not felt for any man since Keoki's father. She wandered among the guests while waiting for him to return to the house and find her. But he didn't return, and it was only minutes before she was due to be in the library. She felt suddenly shattered he had not come after her. Not the right time or the right place? That had been the only reason she had run away from him. Had he been sorry for what had passed between them? His wife and children were very good reasons for him to forget what had happened in the garden.

Syrah was taking heart, feeling her spirits revive. She knew in the marrow of her bones that James felt the same way as she did. It was thrilling to realise that nothing could cool her ardour or quench the sense of love kindled in her after those few minutes, in his arms. They were to be each other's destiny. How? When? Why? It mattered not in the least. That, after all was how destiny worked. New life springing so quickly from the ashes of death was something Syrah could never have expected. Out of her gloom and loneliness a flicker of light and hope. She told herself there was a future, her greatest adventure had to be lived out there, and live it she would. Sadly without Ethan, but with his blessing at least.

It was a few minutes past five o'clock when Syrah approached the library door. Mr Wang and Diana, her arms crossed over Keoki's chest, holding him close to her, gave courage with their smiles. The sort that said, Be brave. Syrah gave them back a look that reassured them she was in control of herself. She faced the confrontation calmly: Caleb, Paula, and three lawyers. Ethan's legacy to be passed on for future generations. Before she pushed open the door she told herself, What does it matter? I can face my mistakes, come to terms with my destiny. Begin again.

Then, feeling as if she was stepping off a cliff, her courage in her hands, Syrah pushed open the door.

Chapter 5

As expected, Ethan bequeathed to his son Caleb the
Richebourg-Conti winery and vineyard, the family house,
all his stocks and shares. Diana had been wrong. Nothing
had been left to Keoki. Syrah listened, feeling as cold as
stone and filled with sadness not for herself but for her
son, that Richebourg-Conti would no longer be a part of
his life. Caleb and Paula had the power to see to that. She
watched her brother and sister-in-law very nearly jump
from their chairs and congratulate each other with hugs
of joy.

Syrah wanted to remain civilised and in some way
wished Caleb and Paula well as the new owners of
Richebourg-Conti. But she was too numbed with grief
for the loss of her father and her former home to move.
The sense of what she had lost was overwhelming. She
could think of nothing except that one lifestyle was over
for her and another would have to begin. The prospect
was too daunting to even contemplate.

She snapped back to attention when Paula turned from
her husband's embrace to face Syrah. In a voice dripping

with condescension, eyes glowing with victory, she declared, 'Now you've heard it, it's official. Richebourg-Conti is ours. I see no need for you to remain here any longer. Please leave the room and *our* estate as soon as you can conveniently gather your son and your friend together.'

Caleb, walking towards the still-seated Syrah, watched her rise from her chair. Even in her grief over the loss of their father, the destruction of her lifestyle, the curtailment of any revenue from Richebourg-Conti, she remained beautiful, vibrant, formidable. Dazzlingly attractive and with a charm exactly like their father's. Seeing so much of Ethan in her took Caleb aback. He felt something for both Syrah and Ethan then that allowed him, for a moment, to forget the years of hatred and hark back to a time when he and his sister both adored their father and love had governed their relationship.

He addressed her then, a hint of softness in his voice. 'If ever you're destitute and need advice, I'll be here for you. This house will never be the same without Ethan, I think we both know that. Paula and I will make it on our own. That said, I'd like you and Keoki to visit us every Christmas Eve and to stay for Christmas dinner. Ethan would have wanted that.'

Paula shot a withering glance at her husband. Turning to Syrah, she declared, 'That will depend on *my* family's plans for the Christmas festivities. I don't think you should see it as an obligation, either on your part or ours.'

During this confrontation, yet again Syrah was made

to realise just how much she'd offended her brother and sister-in-law. Their demonstration in the presence of the family lawyers clearly illustrated that. Caleb's assumption that she would be destitute, and that destitution was the price she must pay for the privilege of making contact with her brother, was horrifying to her. Feeling poleaxed by their hatred of her, Syrah somehow managed, without uttering a word, to walk away from her brother and sister-in-law in a dignified manner. It was no mean feat considering she was inwardly screaming with pain and her mind was spinning with fear of having no family and being poverty-stricken, having to change – *how* to change – her lifestyle.

Syrah's hand was on the door knob when Baskin Coolidge, one of the family lawyers, rose from his chair. 'Syrah, I would advise you to remain here until I have finished reading your father's will. There are several other bequests you should be made aware of and one of them is to your advantage.'

She turned round to look at the group. She had had enough, could think of nothing but running away from the aura of hatred emanating from Caleb and Paula. Baskin Coolidge gave her a smile of encouragement and nodded: an intimation that she should return to her chair. Paula and Caleb looked non-plussed. They had it all, what was there left for Syrah? A gesture and nothing more, assumed Paula, returning to her chair.

Everyone else was seated once more before Syrah reluctantly walked backed across the room. Baskin

Coolidge read out some bequests, all monetary, to old friends, the ever faithful Mr Wang and Richebourg-Conti staff.

Paula was looking smug. There had been nothing in the monetary bequests to Syrah or Keoki. At the same time she was wary because Mr Coolidge had convinced her sister-in-law there was something worthwhile staying for.

Baskin Coolidge had been Ethan's personal lawyer for more than twenty years. He had promised to see that his client's wishes were adhered to. He, as well as Ethan, knew that Caleb and Paula would contest the will and before he even read out the bequest to Syrah, Baskin Coolidge was prepared to do battle for her if need be.

He cleared his throat and then proceeded to read from the papers in his hand: "'And finally, to my beloved daughter Syrah Richebourg-Conti and her son Keoki Richebourg-Conti, I leave the small vineyard Ruy Blas, consisting of seven acres of vines producing an average of sixteen hundred cases of Richebourg-Ruy Blas a year.'"

'No!' shrieked Caleb. Paula, white with rage, shot out of her chair and snatched the document from Baskin Coolidge's hands, wanting to read the bequest with her own eyes.

The lawyer, without uttering a word, merely searched through the stack of papers in front of him and retrieved a copy of the will. He found his place and continued, "'In addition, I leave to Syrah my private wine cellar, my most precious possession.'"

It was evident that Caleb and Paula were trying to bring their rage under some semblance of control. Syrah, overwhelmed by her father's gift to her, felt choked with emotion and sat silently fighting back tears.

'Betrayal even in death!' hissed Paula.

The shock and resentment of the bequest to Syrah and Keoki was evident in Syrah's brother's and sister-in-law's faces; indeed their entire body language displayed hatred. Gone was their elation at Ethan's bequest to them. Their understanding had been he would leave Syrah nothing and instead he had left her the two most precious jewels in his crown.

Caleb rose from his chair, almost exploding with anger. 'I will contest that bequest, Baskin. My understanding has always been that my father would leave nothing to Syrah. Both Paula and I heard that from him many times. I am certain he meant to do just that but was finally too weak-willed. Here is yet further proof that Syrah was Ethan's favourite child. To leave her Ruy Blas and his wine cellar . . . madness! It is part and parcel of Richebourg-Conti and therefore belongs to Paula and myself. Baskin, that bequest is illegal. We have inherited it, not my sister.'

'Ethan will not win this round!' Paula put in. 'We'll drive Syrah away physically if need be. We demand an injunction be placed on the property so she cannot sell it. I want her banned from Ruy Blas and my father-in-law's wine cellar. That sly old fox! He may not have left her as much as a dime in currency but a cellar valued at six million dollars and the finest vines in the Napa Valley . . . they're the heart and soul of Richebourg-Conti.'

Caleb attacked Syrah again after Paula had run out of threats. 'What Dad did was illegal but let's leave that aside for the moment. Your lack of business acumen and ignorance of the wine trade make it impossible for you to administer such assets. You have chosen the life of a spoiled playgirl whose daddy kept her lifestyle going. You've done it before . . . traded in your stake in Richebourg-Conti for the high life. You'll do it again! You will sell off your ill-gotten legacy so you can continue your self-indulgent way of life. Why ever would Dad behave so foolishly? Vindictiveness? Disloyalty to Paula and myself? The selfish destructiveness of a dying man?'

Baskin Coolidge rose from his chair and addressed Caleb and Paula. 'I would strongly advise you, Caleb, and your wife, to come to terms graciously with the bequest made by Ethan to Syrah and Keoki. I can assure you it is fully legal and binding. To contest it would only be costly and counter-productive for all concerned.'

Syrah listened to the ranting and raving of her brother and sister-in-law but it hardly affected her. She was too overcome with gratitude and pride that Ethan should have believed in her enough to have left her his two most precious possessions. He had once entrusted her with a secret: 'I have three keys to my kingdom: Ruy Blas, my wine cellar and you, Syrah.' Then as now she had not quite understood what her father meant. Nor did she understand the ramifications of Ruy Blas being split from

Richebourg-Conti. She was, however, quick to deduce from Caleb and Paula's reaction to the bequest that they did.

Three keys to a kingdom and she one of them. That was all she could think of. After shaking hands with the lawyers Syrah walked from the room without uttering a word to either Caleb or Paula.

She heard the mahogany door shut behind her and stood with her back against it. Syrah took several deep breaths in the hope of calming herself then went looking for Keoki and Diana. She found them in the midst of several of Diana's admirers. When the women's eyes met, Diana skilfully managed to detach herself and Keoki from them and join her friend.

Syrah's first words were to her son. 'Ethan did not forget us! He's left us his most prized possessions: the small vineyard Ruy Blas and his wine cellar. Those gifts are an overwhelming gesture of love for us and trust in me to guard them well, make of them something he would be proud of. I'm sure that's why he did it!'

The three of them hugged each other, not so much from joy as in deep sadness.

James Whitehawk, several vineyard owners and Ira Rudman, standing near the trio, could hardly help but overhear Syrah. James's eyes met hers and something loving passed between them. It prompted him to go to her.

'It was impossible not to overhear that you have inherited Ruy Blas,' James told her and then led her to the group of other vineyard owners he was with.

It was their enthusiasm over her being the new owner of Ruy Blas that finally raised her spirits. She had arrived at Richebourg-Conti without a friend and expecting nothing and was leaving with a handful of desperate wine men who were willingly, insistently, offering to help her and her small vineyard in anyway they might. She listened to them and felt such pride that Ethan had left her Ruy Blas. It was revered by wine men the world over. One of the men, Renzzo Polito, a vineyard owner from Tuscany, one of the many wine elite who had flown in from abroad, asked humbly, 'When you are settled in, might I walk through Ethan's wine cellar with you?' No one until then had mentioned Ethan's private cellar.

'Yes, I would be happy for any of you to tour the cellar with me,' answered Syrah, confused by the request since she had not as yet come to terms with owning it.

It was Ira Rudman, having heard the offers of help from vineyard owners who could hardly help themselves, the respect they showed Syrah as the new owner of Ruy Blas and Ethan's wine cellar, who spoke next. He went to stand next to her, placed a protective arm round her shoulders. He saw how vulnerable she was and grabbed his moment to capitalise on her misery and confusion.

'Syrah, you have always made it clear that you chose a way of life other than the wine world. Ethan in his generosity has inflicted a burden on you that you are hardly qualified to handle. Give me first refusal on the vineyard and the wine cellar and I'll see that you never regret it. We can dispose of the matter immediately and you and Keoki can return to the lifestyle you're used to.'

The men around her fell silent. Ira's assumption that Syrah would want to sell off her legacy as soon as possible surprised them all. Looks of disapproval were etched sharply on their faces. Their expressions and the discreet signal from James that she should immediately decline Ira's offer could hardly be ignored.

Syrah studied the face of the millionaire property developer. She knew him so well, knew how he'd tried to cultivate a business arrangement with Ethan who'd dismissed Ira's schemes for Richebourg-Conti out of hand. Why, she wondered, did he want Ruy Blas? How did he know these wine men? She sensed she was missing something. Of course she was. Being away from the wine world for so long she was unaware that Ira was ruthlessly buying as many of the bankrupt or nearly ruined vineyards and wineries in the Napa Valley as he could as soon as they came on the market.

The warmth of love James emanated towards her, the support of these near strangers who had loved Ethan, each of them in their own way making her feel part of the wine world, affected her strongly. She gently removed Ira's arm from round her shoulders.

'Now why would I do that, Ira?'

'Because it would be a good deal for you. You have to sell to someone so it might as well be me.'

'Why do you assume I intend to sell off Ruy Blas and Ethan's wine cellar?'

Ira burst into laughter. Calming himself, he told her, 'Because you're a playgirl, not a businesswoman. Because you may have been born into the wine world but you have never worked in it nor shown any interest in doing so. Being Ethan's daughter will smooth your way but never make you the Master Of Wine he was. I warn you, Syrah, you are in no position to make such a rash decision: a woman without a work ethic, no knowledge of the wine business, a woman without business acumen and a father no longer here to pick up the tab for her. For friendship's sake, I'll leave the offer open.'

A shark nibbling at her flesh was how she saw Ira and his offer then. Fear that he might eat her alive gave her a rush of adrenaline. Raising her chin that little bit higher, she told him, 'Hearing your offer, and the reasoning that allowed you to assume I would want to rid myself of my legacy as soon as possible, has made me come to one realisation: Ethan believed that I would do right by his gifts to Keoki and me. He understood that I would never have the heart to sell them off to anyone, least of all a property developer who would chew up his vines and spit them out in favour of some vulgar skyscraper condominium.'

With that she turned her back on him and after shaking the hands of all the men in the group surrounding her, told them, 'Thank you for your kind offers of help.'

'You're leaving?' asked James.

'Yes, the sooner the better. We're only staying long

enough to gather our things,' she answered him.

'I'll drive you to the air strip,' he offered.

A short time later, James was standing next to his car at the entrance to the family house. He watched Syrah, Diana and Keoki walk down the stairs flanked by floral tributes to Ethan. He could hardly keep from staring at Keoki, so handsome and exotic-looking with an aura of sweetness that touched James's heart. Syrah's child! How he wished he had been the father of this love child of hers. The boy looked up at him, their eyes met and a bond was immediately forged between them. James walked up several stairs to greet Keoki and shake his hand.

'I'm one of your mother's oldest friends. We grew up together. Our fathers were good friends too, the best. I loved Ethan as I loved my own father. Come along, I'm going to drive you to your mom's plane.'

And with those words said, James slid his arms around the boy and gave him a hug, took his hand and then Syrah's. With Diana alongside Syrah, arms linked, they left the house of mourners behind them.

Once settled in James's car for several minutes they were silent. Only the sound of gravel crunching under the tyres and a bird singing somewhere in a tree broke the silence. The four of them were lost in their own thoughts. Finally it was James who broke the silence. 'Syrah, as you're the new owner of Ruy Blas, I think I should tell you some things that are going on in the Valley. They might influence you in your handling of it.'

James could see Syrah, Keoki leaning against her, in the rear-view mirror. His heart raced that little bit faster. He could feel in the marrow of his bones that Syrah was coming home. Ethan had given her the chance and he was certain she would grasp it in both hands. Hadn't Ethan told James often enough that Syrah, in the final analysis, had a passion for the vine that Caleb and Paula would never have? Only she had never as yet come to terms with it. James looked briefly at Diana, who smiled back at him. For a few seconds he was dazzled by her beauty, that special charisma that helped to make her the great actress she was. It was that smile of approval more than anything else that spurred him on.

'You've been away from the Valley and what's going on here for a very long time. Things are very difficult financially for the small independent growers. That will include you now. Out from under the umbrella of Richebourg-Conti, and without its support and Caleb and Paula's help, you will be one of the smaller vineyards – though granted the most prestigious one in all of California, an independent with great power. If you keep Ruy Blas, remember that for most of the time the vineyard will be an uphill battle to run but with monumentally exciting rewards waiting at every harvest.

'Syrah, men like Ira have for the last few years been pushing their way into the Napa Valley and buying most anything they can get their hands on. Ira Rudman has been seen around Richebourg-Conti frequently. He's been cultivating a friendship with Caleb and Paula, but never got to first base with Ethan. He wanted none of the diversification plans Caleb and Paula dreamed up with Ira. Your brother and sister-in-law have been feeding information to Ira about which of the smaller vineyards are in a bad way or going down, the banks foreclosing. Rudman has bought up too much vine-rich land and now we're all concerned.'

'The bastard!' exclaimed Diana.

'You can be sure he has something big in mind. Ira never does things in a small way. How stupid and mean of Caleb and Paula,' declared Syrah.

'Wine is in our blood. We were born into the industry. Whatever you do about Ruy Blas, I'm sure it will be the right thing. Think long and hard on what you want for you and Keoki, the life you want to lead and where the world of wine fits into it. And remember, I am here for you if ever you need my help.'

'James, you always were my knight in shining armour,' she said. He saw the softness of love for him in her eyes and heard it in the sound of her voice.

'And you have always been my Lady of Shallott. Those were the happiest days of my life,' he told her.

The airfield was in sight and Syrah's tangerine bi-plane stood under the afternoon sun like a rare butterfly. Everyone fell silent as James drove across the grass towards the plane. He stopped the car close to the double-winged aircraft. No one made a move to leave. It was several minutes before Diana turned round in her seat to face Keoki, 'Well, sport, let's you and me climb into our flying gear and get settled in our seat,' she suggested to the boy.

Still looking at Syrah and Keoki through the rear-view mirror, James watched the boy kiss his mother's cheek before he leaped from the seat and flung the door open. Syrah, still in her mourning clothes, followed her son from the car. James, now standing beside her, placed a hand on her shoulder. It held her back from following her son and Diana. Syrah and James did not speak. Being alone together for a few minutes seemed enough for them. Syrah climbed into her flying suit while he watched her.

Once dressed she turned to him and said, 'You are all I have, all I trust, and your being here for me now makes me wonder why I ever ran away from you.'

'Foolish youth. Shall we leave it at that for now and forever?' he answered her.

'You always did make everything easy for me,' she told him.

The love that shimmered between them was too intense even to contemplate. The sexual attraction so strong it was impossible to deny it. For each of them it was too personal, too deep, to do anything about at that moment. James, taking both her hands in his, raised them to his lips and kissed them. Syrah had never felt so loved except by Ethan.

'There's so much more I'd like to say. I don't know where to begin,' Syrah told him.

'Nor I.'

'Our time will come.'

'Yes, but until then it would be best for you to take immediate action to protect yourself and your vineyard. The Ruy Blas manager and his staff of vineyard workers, who have been working together for as long as I can remember, are under the Richebourg-Conti umbrella. I think you should assume that now Caleb and Paula own Richebourg-Conti they will go after your legacy too. They need Ruy Blas, it's the flagship of Richebourg-Conti.

'The first thing Caleb will do is to make the Ruy Blas workforce redundant or at the very least snatch them back to work on the Richebourg-Conti vineyards. If that were to happen your vineyard and Ethan's cellar would be doubly vulnerable to sabotage, thievery, court orders and claims by your brother. I believe he will stop at nothing to seize your legacy back from under his control.'

'What shall I do?' asked Syrah, who realised James was talking good sense. She *did* have to protect Ruy Blas. Running back to Malibu to mourn the death of her father and think about what to do with her life and her legacy was not reacting responsibly to Ethan's grand gesture of love. Of course she would have to protect her inheritance, even if she didn't know how.

James was acutely aware of the anxiety he was causing Syrah. It showed on her face. He reached out to sweep a strand of her hair from her cheek and caress it with the back of his hand. She leaned into his hand and once more they were aware of how close they were to each other. How much richer their lives had instantly become now that they had once more found each other. That realisation did nothing to comfort them. It would also complicate things for both of them.

James ignored the passion he felt for Syrah and addressed the problem at hand. 'If you would like me to, I will go directly from here to Ruy Blas and find the manager, Henri Chagny, and the vineyard workers. I have been close to these men all of my life. I know many of them well, men from my own tribe who sit on the same tribal council as I do. They have their own loyalties to the land and the vines. If I go to them as soon as I see you off and suggest they resign from Richebourg-Conti, who pay them as Ruy Blas workers, their resignations effective immediately, I believe you'll be able to hire them in your own name and place them under contract to Richebourg-Ruy Blas. As the new owner you have every right to do that. The vineyard would then be run as it always was before Ethan's death.'

James's suggestion seemed so right. His help gave Syrah a focus on her legacy and a new understanding of how she would have to fight for the vineyard to keep it. A shiver of excitement travelled through her entire body and she came to terms with the fact that she loved the land, the vine and the grape. With a sense of belonging, she realised she had come home.

There was a tremor in her voice when she told him, 'Please do that for me. Get the men to stay and work for me as they did for Ethan. And, James, please keep a watch on what's going on at Ruy Blas until I can straighten out my affairs in Malibu. Getting my head round the changes

I will need to make is not going to be easy. I'll call you as soon as I am back there.'

Their numbers were hurriedly exchanged on scraps of paper furnished by James. They kissed just once: deeply, passionately, urgently. Then Syrah broke away from his embrace and into a run. James watched her check that Keoki and Diana were safely seated before she put on her flying jacket and climbed into the forward cockpit. James pulled the chocks from under the wheels, the plane's motor burst into life and the propeller sputtered into action. Syrah taxied away from James and the three of them waved farewell to him. James raced to his car and was away from the field before Syrah had even taken off the ground. At breakneck speed he drove to Ruy Blas. Instinct told him she would circle her vineyard before flying away.

He arrived at the vineyard only minutes before Syrah swept out of the sky over Ruy Blas. She circled it twice and then, flying low over the vines dipped the wings from side to side. Her long white silk scarf drifted lazily down from the sky. James ran to catch it in mid-air. He pressed it to his lips. By then she was gone, flying into a waning sun.

Chapter 6

Circling over Ruy Blas, *her* vineyard, Syrah's thoughts were not of what she had reaped from her father's death but what she had lost: a man who'd loved her for everything she was and was not, for everything she could be. James and what had happened to them in an instant in the garden brought new hope to her that at the direst time of her life someone was watching over her. She relived once more that recognition of an intense and exciting love they'd had for one another, the passion of two hearts beating as one.

Dropping her scarf to James, a gesture of wanting to leave him with something of herself to contemplate, was all she could manage as she flew away from the Valley to Malibu. Her preoccupation with the loss of her father had too great a hold on her, was in a certain sense crippling her. Flying through the blue, cloudless sky, fragments of the last few days seemed miraculously to come together in her head: the loss of Ethan was going to be temporary; she sensed her father would always be with her, a part of her life kept very much alive as long as she and Keoki had Ruy Blas. And James? A temporary parting? Yes! It was so clear to her that they would find each other and a way to be together in love. Doesn't destiny demand it? she asked herself, and was certain that it did.

It was Diana who drove them from the field where Syrah kept her plane, Keoki was asleep and the two women made the journey to Syrah's house in silence. Only when they arrived and Diana pulled off the road and into the drive did they speak.

'Would you like me to stay with you for a few days?' asked Diana.

'No. I've taken so much of your time when you should be in rehearsal. How ever will I be able to thank you for seeing Keoki and me through this terrible time?' Then Syrah burst into tears. Her emotional stamina was drained. There was nothing she could do about that. Both women were aware that time and distance away from the dreadful days and nights they had been through would be the only healer.

They hugged each other and Diana awakened Keoki just as Melba Morissey arrived through the wooden gate. The housekeeper took Keoki in hand and, placing an arm round Syrah's shoulder, walked them to the wide door which she opened with her latch key. Diana watched the house burst out of darkness and into light. She waved to Syrah and drove away, relieved that Melba would take over and pamper her friend and Keoki.

For Syrah, being home and surrounded by her happy-go-lucky life and familiar things was an uplifting experience. Suddenly she was confronted with her old lifestyle and the fun it had been filled with. It felt good – frivolous, but oh, so very good. Ethan's death, the dreadful Caleb and Paula and their greed, were a whole world away. What had that to do with her life and the way she wanted to live it?

For the next few days she caught up on her sleep and walked the beach, putting friends and social engagements aside. She and Keoki slipped into their old lifestyle as if it were going to go on like that forever. Syrah did not call James. She knew he would understand that she needed time to evaluate what had happened to her. But then he didn't call her either. With the post every morning came household bills. She never even bothered to open them. That was too much like real life intruding on her private world.

Finally one morning Syrah had come to terms with dealing with her finances. She wrote cheques, filed the invoices marked 'Paid' and forgot about them. Several days later she was astounded by a call from her bank. Her current account was overdrawn and the bank demanded a deposit of funds to be made immediately to cover her overdraft. Such a demand had never in the past been a problem, either for the bank or Syrah, both had known it would only take a phone call to Ethan Richebourg and any temporary financial embarrassment was over. But there was no longer an Ethan Richebourg nor an account in his name for funds to be drawn from. The problem loomed large for both the bank and Syrah:

Ethan Richebourg's support was gone forever.

Syrah's leisurely and stress-free world came crashing down around her. Pressure to wake from her inertia and take some action began to mount for her. She was without a penny of cash reserves, had a nervous bank manager who believed the bank had always been too lenient with her financial affairs. The result: Syrah was cash poor and in serious debt as she had never been before. A call from Baskin Coolidge to say that Caleb and Paula had been advised Ethan's will was legal and binding, and any action through the courts would almost certainly end in failure, made it impossible even to think she might be able to return to her old carefree way of living. Suddenly she was beset with serious responsibilities.

Her immediate action was to borrow twenty-five thousand dollars from Diana so she could make good the cheques she had written and there was enough cash for her day-to-day living expenses. That in itself was embarrassing. Although Diana made it as easy as possible to smooth over her friend's having to ask for financial help, it did not come easy to Syrah, even from a best friend. She felt uncomfortable and rather foolish that she had, all her life, not interested herself greatly in money. On that front worse was yet to come. She was forced to look at the enormous debts her once considerable credit had allowed her to accumulate: the mortgage on the Malibu property, a portfolio of bad investments that needed propping up on a long and continuous basis. Lack of income of any sort was the most disturbing of her problems; second, lavish purchases that she could no longer afford to pay off. The lack of cash flow to keep her lifestyle going was forcing her into a world she had never experienced.

She found it difficult to accept that this was to be her life from now on. Confused, not knowing where to turn or what to do, she did the only thing she could do, called on her financial advisers: her bankers and her father's accountants. And suddenly they were no longer there for her as they had been all her adult life. She was made to understand that Caleb's curtailing her income from Richebourg-Conti had ruined her. Their only advice was that she should liquidate her assets, pay off the debts she had, which would more than likely push her into bankruptcy, and begin afresh. In other words, get a job and live within her means.

Syrah slid into despair as easily as going down a water slide. It was then, in her darkest moment, that Caleb called on her. He arrived at her door, unannounced and without Paula. Her spirits were raised by the sight of him. Why was he there? Had he forgiven her? Had he forgiven their father for loving her? Was it true that blood was thicker than water? Was what had happened between them at Richebourg-Conti a bad dream conjured up by the death of Ethan? Those were the thoughts running through her mind as her brother walked through the drawing room on to the wooden deck overlooking the beach where Syrah, in a bathing suit, sat sunning herself while contemplating her grave situation.

'Whatever are you doing here, Caleb?' she asked, only to realise the moment she had uttered the words that they, as well as her tone, were hardly welcoming.

'Well, I'm glad you see fit to come straight to the point. I might say you're looking like hell warmed over. Are you ill?' he asked.

'That wasn't very welcoming, I agree. Sorry, I'm not myself at the moment. Do sit down. I'll tell Melba to get us some cool drinks and a bowl of fruit,' she told her brother as she rose from the chaise she had been lying on and wrapped a sarong round her.

Caleb did not take a chaise but a wooden chair placed at a round stone table looking out towards the ocean. The sky was a hazy mother-of-pearl colour streaked with clear blue gashes made by a soft warm breeze trying to push the haze away and out to sea. He watched some of the beautiful people who lived on the beach walking, or jogging, along the water line and despised them as he did his sister for this luscious and frivolous life that was spent in such a laid-back manner.

When he had walked in on her, Syrah had looked distressed yet still beautiful. Captivating in fact. He had always been proud of her beauty, knowing it to be that rare kind that comes not from vanity but something deeper that not many women could match. All his life he had wanted some of that to rub off on him, but it never had. Caleb sighed. She and her beauty, her charisma, had ruined their lives. The love that some siblings were able to achieve and keep for always had never happened for them. Syrah should have made an effort, he told himself, and liked her even less today because in his eyes she never had.

She returned to the sun deck dressed in white: a pair of wide-legged trousers, a white shirt with long sleeves rolled up and its tails tied at her midriff. A sliver of tanned flesh showed there that he found oddly tantalising. Caleb had missed nothing: she had brushed her hair and dabbled with her face and she was barefoot. Just looking at her Caleb knew he had been right in telling Paula not to come with him though it had caused yet another row between them. Their rows almost always had something to do with either Ethan or Syrah.

She took the chair opposite her brother. Almost immediately she sensed a tension between them but mercifully this meeting was on her territory not Caleb's. She gained some strength from that thought. He remained silent. She simply didn't know what to say to him. The tension was broken when Melba arrived with a jug of freshly squeezed orange juice and a glass bowl of luscious-looking fruit. Brother and sister remained silent when the housekeeper left them to return shortly with plates, silver forks and knives, and white linen napkins.

Syrah scraped back her chair and took several steps away from the table to lean against the balustrade. Facing him, she finally broke the silence. 'What are you doing here, Caleb? And without Paula at your side? Is this to be some sort of a reconciliation between brother and sister, possibly an apology for the many cruel and twisted things you had to say to me at Dad's funeral? No! The look on your face says I have it all wrong as usual.'

She was fighting back tears. Not one of the things she had said to her brother had been what she had meant to say. In her heart she wanted him suddenly to transform himself into a loving sibling who adored her as her father had. To come to her aid. To beg that they should begin again and learn to love each other. That had been the case once when they had been children before their egos had divided them.

A nice thought that could never be realised because Syrah recognised disapproval, dislike even, in Caleb's eyes. Quite possibly even hatred. She sensed she had had little choice but to take a defensive position with her brother. It had been instinctive and, she realised, while still gazing at him, a matter of self-preservation.

Syrah poured the orange juice into two large crystal goblets and handed one to Caleb. He took the glass and drank from it. After placing it on the table he told her, 'I thought it was best to come here and make you an offer you can hardly refuse, rather than dealing through our respective lawyers. I want the legacy Ethan left you. I *need* it. Richebourg-Conti *needs* it. You don't. It will be a heap of baggage on your back whose weight will bring you to your knees and eventually crush you.

'I'm prepared to give you a substantial monthly allowance for the remainder of your life, one that will keep you in the style to which you are accustomed, if you will sign over the rights of your legacy to me and never return to Richebourg-Conti. I have taken the liberty of having the papers drawn up,' he told her as he withdrew them from the inside pocket of his jacket.

'Never!' she exclaimed, barely above a whisper. That too was instinctive because she certainly did need that kind of money, and the security of a financial future.

'Did I hear you say *never*?' asked Caleb.

'Yes, I guess you did.'

'Wrong answer, Syrah. I suggest you think again and then sign this document.'

'I hear a threatening tone in your voice, Caleb. Are you warning me I'd better sign or else? Or else what? Just what more do you think you can do to me you have not already done?'

'If you do not at the very least consider my offer and call your lawyer to join us in a meeting to hash out the details, I will call Paula and tell her there is no deal. She will then call the bank and tell them to call in your considerable outstanding loans and every one of your creditors. You will ruin yourself, have to sell off everything to keep Ethan's legacy and watch the grapes rot on the vines. Even your precious plane will be gone. You're no wine maker nor a worker. You've no funds to run your holding, and not a clue about business. I want that legacy, Syrah, and I mean to get it. You will have to sell and I know one thing for sure: you will never sell it outside the family because Ethan would turn over in his grave if you did and you couldn't bear that.'

She rose from her chair and walked round the table to

stand next to her brother. Something had snapped within her from stress, deep grief, the aura of hatred and greed surrounding Caleb. She watched him rise from his chair. A moment of madness came over her then. Passion and self-respect rose in her, a sense of self-worth took her over. Her hand shot out and she slapped Caleb several times hard across his face, first on one cheek then the other, swift as a serpent's darting tongue.

She trembled with rage. Her mouth dry, she could barely speak but when she did she told her brother, 'Out! Out now before I count to ten. Because if you're still here then I will call the police and have you physically removed. Stay out of my life, Caleb, and off my land. Yes, *my* land. Out of *my* wine cellar. Until you arrived here with your lust for my legacy, I had no idea of what I wanted to do with it. I wasn't even thinking about it. That's no longer the case. Always remember, you greedy bastard, it was *you* who made my mind up for me. You who reminded me I am not the woman you think I am but my father's daughter. You will rue this visit for as long as you live.' And Syrah began counting, 'One, two . . .'

She watched Melba silently hand her brother a white handkerchief which he placed against the trickle of blood oozing from his nose. Syrah stood her ground and watched her housekeeper usher him from the terrace and out of the house to his car.

She was shaken by the confrontation but Caleb had driven her into a corner of despair she could no longer bear. To retaliate as violently as she had quite traumatised her. Her feelings were mixed and foreign to her. She was feeling in control of herself and her life as she had never been before and yet she was like a new-born babe, living in the moment and not knowing or even thinking what to do next.

Caleb was as good as his word. One enormous problem after another fell upon Syrah like great stones. Weighed down by them and with not enough time to contemplate them or what to do with Ruy Blas, she let things drift for several weeks. The only bright light on her horizon being that, although for the moment she had abandoned her vineyard and cellar, James had not. He was carrying out the plan he had mapped out for her and keeping away from Syrah so that she might have the space and time she needed to heal from Ethan's death.

It was during those few weeks after Caleb's visit that the many condolence letters from friends and business associates of her father's in the wine industry, containing offers of help when she was ready to enter the wine world and take up her father's gauntlet, made Syrah realise how much a part of her her legacy was. The words of those men and women who had loved and respected Ethan for the man and Master of Wine he had been made such a profound impression on her that she began to understand how much she needed to take control of her life and once more become a part of the Napa Valley. She must find a way to make a niche for herself and Keoki in the name of great wine, and to emulate Ethan's life's work.

So many times during those stressful weeks in Malibu her thoughts turned to James: sensual longings to be with him in lust and love, to feel his body next to hers, even the scent of the man, were things she conjured up in the loneliness of the night. Yet she never called him. She did not want to mix up the need she felt for him with love or sexual passion, not until she was able to make an attempt at sorting out the mess that was her life at the moment. He never called from the Valley and she loved him more for that – that he knew without being told that she needed time to mourn Ethan and get her life in order; that she would call him when she was free and ready to move on in his direction. She had walked away from him and his love once long ago. She wanted to be sure of her feelings for him now because she knew she could never do that again.

Then one morning she woke and felt a strength that she had always had but which had deserted her with Ethan's death. She was herself once more and feeling she had come out of some dark and dismal place into the light. It was around half past six in the morning, Keoki and Melba were still asleep in their rooms. The sun was out and there was a fresh breeze coming off the Pacific. There was hardly a soul out on the beach. Syrah donned a pair of loose white linen trousers and a T-shirt, a wool jumper over that, and walked from her bedroom down the stairs to the beach. Barefoot, she ran across the sand to the water's edge and broke into a run. The sound of the waves, a steady mesmerising pulse and the scent of the ocean filled her heart and soul. They seemed to energise her, spur her on. She ran faster, faster, and felt a sheer excitement at being alive – as she had never felt before except possibly when she was in her plane flying solo over the ocean, diving from great heights and sweeping just barely above the tops of the waves only to climb steeply up, up, back into the clouds.

A sense of joy was hers. Laughter had once again entered her life. She ran in and out of the shallows and the cold water caught the cuffs of her trousers which flapped against her ankles. Still on the run, she pulled her jumper off and tied it around her waist and kept running. Other runners and joggers appeared on the beach and by the time Malibu had really woken she was running up the stairs to her house and into the kitchen, out of breath but riding high on adrenaline and the joy of being alive.

Keoki was having his breakfast. Melba, busy pouring milk, had only to look at Syrah to know she had returned to them whole and her own self. She rushed over to her son. Throwing her arms around him, she kissed him again and again until giggles of pleasure erupted from them both.

'Pancakes! Lots of your thin luscious pancakes drenched in butter and maple syrup – I'm famished. Pancakes for us all and after that a family conference. I'll be back from my shower in a flash,' she told her housekeeper and son.

In the shower she thought about James and her erotic

feelings for him. Why wasn't he here in the shower with her? She caressed her breasts, silky smooth with bath gel. It felt so good to be fondled. In her misery of the last weeks she had nearly forgotten how good it was to be alive, passionate to live out the excitement of just being in lust and love.

Out of the shower Syrah went directly to the telephone next to her bed and rang James. His mobile telephone was switched off. She rummaged through her handbag and found the office number at Ruy Blas. Henri Chagny answered. No James was not there but Henri expected him and would give him a message.

'Is everything OK with Ruy Blas?' she asked.

'Yes, under control. James checks in every day and the vineyard is carrying on as usual. We appreciate all that he is doing for us, the payroll he meets every week and the running expenses. There have been a few disturbances from Richebourg-Conti on Caleb's orders but we managed to solve the problems. I will have James call you as soon as we hear from him.'

Syrah slipped into a terry-cloth robe and, still towel drying her hair, marched through the house to the kitchen where she dropped the towel into the laundry basket and took a seat at the table. Melba placed a stack of pancakes on the table and mother and son dived at them with their forks while Melba sat down.

All the while they chatted over breakfast, Syrah's mind kept wandering away from the conversation and dwelling on thoughts of James and what he was doing for her at

Ruy Blas. He had taken on a great deal for her.

Three pancakes down the telephone rang. Syrah jumped from her chair to answer it. Instinct told her it was James. Walking from the kitchen with the cordless telephone she heard him telling her, 'Every day since you left I've been waiting for your call. Are you well? Keoki too?'

The moment she heard his voice she was filled with love for him. 'Fine, we're both fine. James, I know how much you're doing for me, Henri told me. I have to know why? What, if anything, do you expect in return?'

He hesitated before he answered. She somehow sensed she had just posed the most important question he would ever have to answer; that what he did answer would govern their respective lives from that day onward. She heard him give a nervous cough and finally clear his throat. She imagined the tears coming to his eyes, and closed her own to try and calm herself.

A slight tremor in his voice, he told her, 'For love and a lifetime of loving you.'

Any questions Syrah might have had about his motives or his personal life vanished instantly from her mind. They were no longer relevant. Only that he loved her. Overwhelmed by his declaration, her own sense of excitement and erotic passion for James surfaced. That love and sensual attraction had been mutual! Life was changing for her at such a dizzying pace she had no time to play love games. She merely blurted out, 'In the garden, when you put your arms around me, an instant sense of love that I know will go on forever overwhelmed me. That's why I ran away. It's something so precious, we must take great care with it. I know you feel the same way.'

'Yes. I never stopped loving you. Though I made a life without you, you were always there. I believed in the depths of my being you would come back to me,' he told her.

'James, all that money you're putting into Ruy Blas – I'm so grateful to you but I'm not used to taking financial advantage of anyone, let alone a man with whom I am in love and who is in love with me. My affairs are in a dreadful state. If I'm to keep and run Ruy Blas, move back to the Valley, which is my intention, I must find a way to finance the vineyard so you need not carry on lending me money. I don't want anything to get in the way of the love that is growing between us, and certainly nothing as crass as taking advantage of it. You do understand?'

'Of course. But until you are able to sort out your affairs and no longer need me to fund Ruy Blas, I will carry on playing its banker.'

'I know nothing of your life, can you afford to help me like this?' asked Syrah hesitantly.

'Not for much longer. But . . . I must see you, talk to you about my present life. It's not so straightforward as I would like it to be.'

Chapter 7

Diana lived in Beverly Hills; possibly the smallest, most understaffed house in Beverly Hills. People envied her English garden, and lawns, her tennis court and cricket pitch; considered the house itself, tucked away behind flowering shrubs and trees, to be enchanting. It had a reputation for being very private and off bounds as a party place.

Ira had bought her the house, which had been extraordinarily expensive. He had insisted upon her accepting it as a gift. 'An expression of love,' he had told her. 'In admiration of your beauty, your unique talent as a great actress, and because I want you always to be living well and close to me.'

The house had five bedrooms and baths, a large kitchen, a long rambling drawing room with French doors that led on to the terrace and garden, a swimming pool and walled kitchen garden. The dining room had been turned into a library but was still used on the rare occasions when Diana did entertain. One of the bedrooms had been turned into a gym, another given over to Keoki.

A third, her own, was enormous and overlooked the pool and gardens that rambled charmingly away from the house, to walks through rose arbours and to a folly.

There was hardly a day that went by when Diana did not remind herself to be grateful for her house. The English matinee idol who had built it fifty years before had created for himself a home that was a corner of England, and not Hollywood-style. Diana clearly loved her house and spent a great deal of time in it.

She had no housekeeper but a houseman, Willoughby. He was a jack-of-all-trades and keeper of her life. A man in his fifties, he had been an actor in B movies but not, sadly, a successful one and so became a dresser for better actors than himself. When the young Diana George won the first of her Oscars, Willoughby recognised in her a great artist. Over the years they became friends and when she became a stage actress as well as a screen star he offered her his services. He was wizard at running her life.

Everyone liked Willoughby who turned out to be more extraordinary than anyone had given him credit for. Even Ira. Willoughby was devoted to Diana, impressed by Ira, adored Syrah and Keoki, and was always in love with some young man who was at all times kept by him but far from Diana and her world. These young men were Willoughby's secret vice, one everyone knew about but never confronted him with. Willoughby's entire purpose in life was to remove the mundane from Diana's, which he did admirably.

She was watching her houseman who stood in the garden talking to Rachel the gardener. A woman in her mid-fifties, she had been working on the garden for the past thirty years. Rachel had come with the house. It had been a condition of sale. Diana's greatest pleasure was to work alongside her in the vegetable and herb patch. The marvellous thing about this odd couple, who lived in staff quarters over the garages, was that they were never intrusive. They respected Diana's privacy, rather snobbishly enjoyed her being a theatre and Hollywood star without playing the celebrity game. Unbeknown to her they kept scrap books of her achievements as well as her celebrity life on Ira's arm in Tinseltown Society.

Diana was constantly bemused by the couple who were most respectful, formal even, with each other. She placed the script she was reading in her lap and closed her eyes. The sun felt good. It soothed her somewhat shattered nerves. The weeks since Ethan's death, being steeped in Syrah's profound sadness and Keoki's loss of the only real male figure in his life, had not been easy. She had been friends with Syrah and Ethan even before Keoki had been born and bore her own sadness at losing the old man too. She had loved him as Syrah's father, he had adored her as a great actress and his daughter's best friend. Their relationship had been as close as a family tie.

Diana and Syrah were the sisters neither of them had been born with. They had seen each other through traumatic events: affairs, Keoki's birth, the years Diana had been blinded by love for Ira. Those times played through her mind as she sat in a wicker chaise next to the pool wearing a large straw hat. She had done very well for herself, this thirty-year-old actress known for her intelligence, exceptional beauty and talent. From humble beginnings, her roots still went deep. Poor, just above survival level, backwoods farming people from the bible belt were her earliest influences. For all her fame and wealth and success, there remained in her a vestige of backwoods farming ideology that at all times kept her feet firmly on the ground.

Diana's rise to celebrity status had not come easily and when it did arrive she lived modestly, saved and invested her money. There had been tips from Ethan about investing and through the years with Ira she'd had access to many more. He had wanted her to have money. Believed that great wealth brought power. So she'd learned from him how to make money and how to keep it. She knew to the very penny how much she was worth but for Diana it was paper money, to play with as she saw fit.

When she finally did walk out on Ira it left her emotionally fragile for some time. She no longer felt the pain of the betrayal he had so publicly inflicted upon her with a nineteen-year-old model he had flaunted for all the world to see while Diana was still living in his house. The gossip columns had made a meal of the very private life of Diana George. She had loved him completely, unconditionally, and for all the years they'd lived together, believed that he loved her in the same way. Now, sitting in the sun, she could remember dispassionately the things that had been so good between them. And the bad things. 'No regrets,' she said aloud, and picked up the script she was reading.

It was a good script and there was a part in it on offer to her. Some time later, still lost in it, she felt a momentary chill. Looking up, she saw Ira standing before her blocking the sun. She leaped from the chair and the script fell on to the grass.

Ira grabbed her by the shoulders. 'I didn't mean to startle you?'

'Well, you have, Ira. And what are you doing here anyway?'

'I wanted to talk to you, it's important to me,' he told her, caressing her hair.

Diana took a step away from him. 'You might have called.'

'I was afraid you wouldn't see me,' he told her as he followed her round the pool towards the house.

'You'd have been right about that. How did you get past Willoughby?'

The passionate feelings she had nurtured so long for this handsome, undeniably sexy man were no longer there. She saw standing before her someone she had loved beyond measure and had watched transform himself from loving human being into someone she could barely recognise. How many times had she tried to save their love affair? Countless. It had been torture for her to see what money and power had done to the man she'd loved.

'I told him you wanted to see me,' was Ira's sheepish reply.

'Since we occasionally move in the same circles, I thought we'd agreed to remain civil in public and nothing in private?' she said.

'Well, I wouldn't have put it exactly like that,' he told her, a disturbing twinkle in his eye.

'I would and I do. Can we leave it at that?'

'You know, I still want you in my life. I've told you that a hundred times and I'll say it again,' he declared as he grabbed her arm in an attempt to stop her.

Diana did stop. She removed her dark glasses. Gazing at him she said, 'What! And be humiliated again by your disloyalty, your pathological womanising. Be constantly exposed to the image of the great land developer multi-millionaire you have made of yourself, your passion for "the deal" and tossing away of genuine generosity. I think not, thank you. And never, but never, come to my house uninvited.'

All that was said not in anger but in a dispassionate voice as cold as steel. It was that tone in her voice that for a brief moment affected Ira more than anything she'd said. Of course he could not be surprised by what she'd had to say about him, it was all true and they both knew it. Ira was a man who knew who and what he was and how to live happily with that. All Diana had had to do was accept him for who he had been and what he had become. He saw her as flawed, her love for him not as strong as she had proclaimed. They had parted because she no longer loved him more than she loved herself. It was that selflessness he had fallen in love with as much as her beauty, fine mind and stardom.

Ira followed her into the kitchen where he watched Diana pour herself a glass of iced tea. He watched her, hand rock steady, showing not a shred of anxiety at his being there.

'A glass of iced tea for me, five minutes of your time and then I'll leave, never to impose myself on you again.'

Diana gazed at him silently. One thing about Ira never changed, he always stood by his word. She turned her back on him and poured a second glass of tea. She handed it to him then placed a plate of freshly made ginger biscuits on the table under an awning off the kitchen and took a chair.

'Five minutes you said? The clock is ticking,' she told him.

'You've changed, become hard.'

'No. Just taken off the blinkers, Ira.'

He laughed. 'Boy, when you make up your mind to play hard ball, you are unbeatable.'

'Now you have four minutes. Hadn't you better get on with it? What do you want?'

'OK, this is serious. I'm here to ask a favour. I want you to convince Syrah to sell me Ruy Blas and Ethan's wine cellar.' As she was clearly about to interrupt him, Ira put up his hand in a signal for her to be quiet and continued, 'Hear me out, *please*, for Syrah's sake. She has no choice but to sell Ruy Blas, it's the only way she can get on with her life. No one will better my offer, her future would be assured.'

'Why this grand gesture of coming to Syrah's rescue? There must be more to your generosity than just seeing she's treated correctly.'

'I couldn't bear for her to be cheated and as you well know she is no businesswoman. Who else will step in and help her? I can assure you her brother won't. Why shouldn't I step in as a gallant? I've always had a soft spot for Syrah. Admired her background: wine aristocracy, the classy lifestyle. I see great potential in the Napa Valley and would love to be the proud owner of Ethan's pet vineyard and wine cellar. Will you help me? You would have done so once without a second thought.'

'That's true, but not any longer. How crass of you to remind me of what we have both lost.'

'We were very good together,' he told her.

A softness, and sexiness came into his voice, a charm she had fallen in love with. She watched his sexuality come to the surface, the way he used it to try and win her over. What for? she wondered. A seduction for a favour? His motives were so blatant she felt he must think her a fool.

Her thoughts were interrupted when he said, 'I'm going to marry. It's time. I wanted it to be you. Neither of us will ever do better for a mate. You should think about that before I find someone else to fit the bill. Who knows? It might even be Syrah. There has always been sexual attraction between us. We fought off deeper feelings because she insisted upon being loyal to you. You left me, allowing that obstacle to vanish.'

'What vanity! And how very typical of you, leaving all options open so you can pluck the best deal for love, sex and marriage Ira-style. Another one of your games: wanting both Syrah and me to round out your life. It will never happen. How clever, how devious you are to seize the moment when she is most vulnerable and I am still weak and burned out from loving you. What lengths would you go to to get me back? What dastardly tricks and ruthless games would you play on Syrah to take over Ruy Blas and Ethan's cellar? Go home, Ira, forget me, I am no candidate for *anything* with you. I know you too well, I've had the best you had to offer. Who and what you have holds no interest for me any more. Will I plead your case to Syrah? I certainly will. But not for your sake, for hers. I will tell her every word of this conversation.'

Ira approached Diana, audaciously, laughter in his eyes and a smile on his lips. He kissed her on the forehead and said, 'That would be the kindest thing you could do for her,' and left.

She sat where Ira had left her for quite a long time. She was not upset by her confrontation with him but wondered how she could ever have loved such a monstrously unloving man. It had been sexual that was for certain. He had been able to awaken in her a sexuality that had been lying dormant, waiting to be released from repressive morality. He had opened her eyes to much she would have missed had she not been with him. But had the love between them been only hers, working overtime? Had she, through all those years with him, lied to herself that he loved her as she did him? Had he always been the man she had seen and heard today? Of course, that had been exactly how it had been. Diana knew now, could face and come to terms with the mess that had been her life with Ira Rudman. She could also accept that though she had truly left him behind her, she had not changed her life or created a new one. Her moments of insight galvanised Diana and she went to the telephone and called her friend.

Syrah was having a terrible day. Every day seemed to be a terrible day for her. Her money problems appeared to become worse week by week. The money she had borrowed from Diana was long since gone. Now it was a matter of selling her possessions and that meant everything, to the last handkerchief if need be, if she was going to work her vineyard and change her life by moving to the Valley. Which was what she intended to do. That in itself posed huge problems but the visit from Caleb had made her mind up for her. Since that morning she had been trying to work out a plan for disposing of her assets. She had tried to keep her stressful situation from Keoki and Melba until she felt the time was right. That time seemed close at hand now.

Syrah heard the sound of Diana's horn. She rushed from the house to open the gates from the highway to her private drive. Short as it was, she had been too slow. Keoki had them partially open. He flung open the door and slid on to and across the seat next to Diana. Godmother and godson kissed each other. His best friend Obi jumped in next to Keoki and they coasted down to the entrance of the house. It was left to Syrah to close the gates.

Seeing the two boys brought a smile to Diana's lips. She did so love Keoki and was always delighted to see Obi, who had an enormous crush on her which she handled in just the right way so as not to embarrass the boy. 'I've brought Chinese for lunch, boys.'

'Our favourite,' they announced in unison, Keoki kissing her once more on the cheek.

The boys, laden down with carrier bags of Chinese takeaway, ran ahead of Syrah and Diana who walked into the house arm in arm. The sight of the two children, their youth and innocence, the carefree world they lived in, charmed the women. In the final analysis was it not goodness and kindness that mattered most? What a shame that as one got older one had to walk through fire of one sort or another to keep those things in the forefront of one's life.

No time for fussing with serving dishes. Once the boys had put out the dinner plates and cutlery, and Melba the napkins, they all sat down and had lunch. The stress that for weeks had showed on Syrah's face seemed to fade away. What she needed was more good times such as these. Occasionally Keoki would look over to his mother and ask, 'All right, Mom?'

The two women saw the boys off with Melba who

was taking them to a Little League baseball game. As they walked back into the house, Syrah said, 'Keoki knows things aren't all right. He's putting up a terrific front, pretending we have no problems.'

'How are the problems?' asked Diana.

'They couldn't be worse. I keep telling myself that as soon as I get a grip on liquidating my assets and organising the paying off of all my debts, I must sit down and talk to Keoki and Melba, explain to them that needs must. This privileged lifestyle is over for us and in order to survive and prosper we are moving to the Valley to work our vineyard. But, it's all so much harder than I thought it would be. I sometimes think I should take the easy way out and sell Ruy Blas. But that's think and not do stuff, a kind of mental masturbation that stops me from pushing on with it. I can't bear to take Keoki away from all he loves.'

'As I told you on the telephone, I had a visit from Ira. Unexpected and unwanted. He simply appeared in my house.'

'I thought it was all over between you?'

'It is,' replied Diana.

'Obviously not for him. He is such a bastard. He'll never get over you being the one to walk out.'

'Syrah, you know how devious he can be. How he'll move mountains to get what he wants. He didn't come just to win me back. He came to beg me to intercede with you to sell him your legacy, claiming you will get no better deal than with him.'

'I turned him down once. Why does everyone assume I want to sell Ruy Blas?'

'Not *want* but *have* to sell, because you need the money,' replied Diana.

'Suddenly my financial affairs are everyone's business. That really irritates me. But what puzzles is why Ira should want my vineyard so badly. He could be after it for Caleb, since I understand they've been trying to do deals together for years. Oh, it's all so confusing! Maybe James will be able to make head or tale of it. He should be here any time now. He's flying down from the Valley. I'm quite nervous about seeing him again.'

Diana watched Syrah place her hands over her eyes and heard her sob. When she removed them her cheeks were stained with tears.

'I love James, not because he's helping me but because when he took me in his arms in the garden at Richebourg-Conti, I felt I had come home to the love I had never found. Love and passion, a sexual attraction that brought us both alive as we have never been with another. I've not seen him since that day we flew away from the vineyard. I'm afraid when he walks through that door it will all have been an illusion and I'll be left with an emptiness of heart and soul.'

'Don't be ridiculous! Remember, I saw you together. And what I saw was a man in love, someone who had found what he'd been searching for. Would you like me to take Keoki for the night?'

Syrah kissed her friend on the cheek and dried her

eyes with a handkerchief. 'He's staying at Obi's house for the night and Melba . . . well, you know Melba. She'll make us dinner and vanish until breakfast. But you are a dear for asking. And, by the way, I don't even know if he wants to spend the night. We never discussed it. I'm not sure if it's a good idea.'

Diana noticed that Syrah had calmed down, was very nearly her old self. She realised that though her friend was coping with her everyday distress, she must get on with moving forward and out of the mess her life was in. This procrastination had to stop! Diana had had no intention of telling her that at that moment but it seemed so imperative she simply blurted it out.

'That's just what I needed to hear. You always give me courage. Remind me to move from the heart as well as the head and get on with my life,' she told Diana.

Chapter 8

Syrah walked through the rooms of her Malibu house wondering what it would be like seeing James here. She could imagine him sitting in that chair, at that table, looking out across the beach to the sea. So transported in her imagination was she that she did not hear the taxi on the drive, missed the sound of the door bell. She felt his presence before she even turned around. He *was* there, standing on the threshold of the open door.

Both of them were hesitant about taking another step towards each other. These were powerful feelings, each of them not wanting to be overwhelmed by what was happening to them, each acutely aware of how starved for love they had been, and for so long. Syrah and James were cautious because they wanted not to bruise each other's heart.

The attraction flaring between them was, if anything, stronger than they'd imagined it to be. The sheer excitement of being in love seemed to be everything for them, gave them time and space, a sense of security strong enough to face their love for each other and savour it.

Syrah was not taken aback by the surprise of seeing him there, nor did she feel any nervous anxiety as she'd thought she might on first seeing him again. In his mere presence, just gazing into his eyes, she sensed his sensual masculinity, his passion, his loving kindness, the adventurer in him with a quiet soul. Her heart did not leap; instead her soul was humbled by the oneness she felt with James. Neither of them spoke, words seemed superfluous, he merely walked across the room to her and took her in his arms.

It was for them then what every man and woman dreams of: love and passion flowing between two people as naturally as a running stream in a wood, as the sun rises and the moon lights up the night. Here was love to be treasured, to be cautious with, not because it was fragile but so that it might continue to grow and blossom, be kept alive for eternity.

To two people entwined in such a love it was more erotic than anything either of them had ever experienced in all their sexually adventurous lives with other partners. It filled their hearts, their souls, and the world stood still for a few minutes. They were aware of having been granted a gift. Someone was watching over them.

James sighed and a smile crossed his lips. Taking both her hands in his, he stood back a pace. He would remember that look of unsullied love for him in her eyes. To the very core of his being, he understood that that was the way she would love him for the rest of his life. He felt his lust for Syrah rising in his loins.

It was Syrah who once more stepped in closer to him and placed her lips upon his, in a kiss to celebrate her passion for James, to express her sexual lust for him. She held nothing back in that kiss, she was giving herself as she had never done to any other man. The intensity of the moment was out of the realm of reason. She broke away from James's lips and called out in ecstasy as she reached a long and strong orgasm. James grabbed her around her waist and lifted her off the floor. She wrapped her legs round him as she unzipped his trousers.

In a passion to have her, to show her how much he wanted her and loved her, he pressed kisses again and again on her lips. He wallowed in the warmth and softness of her mouth. Lost in his lust for Syrah he gave himself over to her, there and then and forever. She was still tearing off his clothes when he impaled her with one powerful thrust. He felt her thighs grip him even tighter and she clung to him with her arms around his neck as he raised the black dress over her head.

The moment James placed his lips over her nipple, Syrah came again in luscious orgasm, the sensation that is incomparable. James backed up against a wall with her still clinging to him. They plunged into an erotic world where the earth, the very world they inhabited, *did* move.

They were in and out of their lust with every thrust. Syrah was alive with passion, holding him tight in an erotic grip that drove him wild with excitement, breathless with desire. They moved easily in their fucking. With every orgasm she surrendered herself more, until she had totally submitted to James in sex and love. At first it had been sexual urgency, lust, that drove them into an erotic nirvana. Syrah felt faint with it. It was then that, without thought or motive, the urgency went out of their love making and they eased into making love, having sex slowly, savouring every leisurely thrust until they came together in one long, unimaginably thrilling orgasm.

Contentment, pure and unadulterated, coursed like blood through their veins. 'You have to know that I have never felt as I do with you: this is joy as I've never known it but once before, when as teenage lovers we discovered sex together. I've always loved you more than any of the other women who came into my life but years ago I gave up fantasising that we would one day be as we are at this moment,' he told her, then kissed her on the lips. He knew that was the kiss that would seal their fate.

'Oh, my dearest heart,' she said as tears slipped from the corners of her eyes to roll down her cheeks. 'I will never leave you again,' she told him.

Together they sat up. Still naked, they hugged each other and remained in that embrace for some minutes, silent except for the warmth of their entwined bodies which seemed to speak volumes.

James retrieved her clothes from the floor and began dressing her. For Syrah it seemed like the most intimate moment of her life. She found his shirt and helped him into it. They took their time dressing each other: caresses, kisses, and an incredible sense of oneness with each other finally took them over.

They rose from the floor together and with arms around each other walked to the sun deck overlooking the beach. The sun was playing on the crest of the waves, turning the Pacific Ocean into rolling, liquid silver. The sky was bright blue with the sun shining in it like a gold shield. There were people on the beach playing volley ball, some running along the water's edge, a few scattered souls sunning themselves.

'I feel we are aliens who have just flown down from another planet. Maybe not a planet, just heaven,' James told her.

Then they both looked away from the scene and burst into laughter because they knew they were somehow outside life and it would always be that way. 'We're the luckiest two people in the world. We've got our second chance,' she told him.

'It won't be easy, not for either of us,' said James, who turned away from her to look out once more across the water.

'No, I don't expect it will. You do know that all this will be gone soon? I've come to accept that. I will have nothing left but Ethan's legacy and I intend to work on that and make a place of my own in the wine world.'

Syrah slipped her arm through James's. Gazing into his eyes she said, 'It doesn't matter. I know you love me not for my money or my lifestyle but for me. Whatever I am, whatever I do. You have always been that way about me and that gives me the strength to begin again, no matter how difficult it may be. I have Keoki and I have you and I have me.'

Together, arms wrapped round each other's waist, they walked into the house to sit together on the suede sofa. 'What's happening in the vineyard?' she asked.

'Ah, well, there's much to tell you about. Over a glass of wine, perhaps?' suggested James.

'Of course! And you must be hungry. You're right, I have been out of this world. Come on, you can select the bottle.'

James selected a bottle of vintage Ruy Blas from the wine cupboard that had been fitted with racks and kept the perfect temperature for wine. Syrah raided the refrigerator and brought out what was left of a glazed baked ham and a wheel of Gorgonzola cheese. She took a French stick from the bread basket and they sat down at the kitchen table, hacking slices of ham and cheese onto broken off pieces of bread while they drank a wine that they agreed was sheer ambrosia.

Neither of them had realised how hungry they were until the first taste of their meal. It was after that, as they munched at the food, that James began talking. 'I think I have to put you in the picture about what's come to light since Ethan's death. What I am about to tell you is not common knowledge. The vast Richebourg-Conti vineyard is debt-ridden without Ruy Blas. As you know, it has always been the jewel in the crown. Richebourg-Conti's debts have to be paid, money must be raised to replant sixty percent of its vines. That money would have come from the profits from Ruy Blas.

'Caleb and Paula have for the last few years been trying to convince Ethan to take Ira Rudman in as an investor, something he flatly refused to do. It's not just your lifestyle but the entire Richebourg-Conti finances that are going into a downward spin. It's been caused by root disease that has been attacking the vines for some considerable time; grandiose secret diversification plans spearheaded by Caleb and Paula behind Ethan's back; property deals with Ira – an international chain of wine outlets that drained Paula's and your brother's cash flow. Caleb and Paula funded these schemes using their personal fortune and stocks in Richebourg-Conti as security, and all without Ethan's knowledge. They knew your father would never allow such gambling.'

James was aware of how pale Syrah had become on hearing this news. Her first reaction was to guess that Ethan had got wind of what was happening. He could no longer trust his son to weather the storm and not lose everything, but he did know that Syrah would. So he'd placed his trust in her, knowing she would never fail him. She pressed her hands over her face and lowered her head. She was racked with anger that Paula and Caleb should be so disloyal to Ethan, and to the generations of Richebourgs, who had made a name in the history of wine that few could challenge.

Raising her head again and removing her hands from her face, she watched in silence as James poured her another glass of wine. She drank from her glass and held it up to the light. '"Liquid rubies, plum-coloured diamonds". How many times have we heard Ethan claim that to be the colour of Ruy Blas wine?' she said, and a smile crossed her face.

She rose from her chair and sliced a thin sliver of ham, a thicker slice of cheese, and broke off another piece of French baguette. Then, going round the table, she placed her food on his plate and drank once more from her glass before sitting down on his lap.

'I have no doubt there's more you have to tell me.' And she placed an arm around his shoulder and leaned against him while she nibbled on her open sandwich.

'Ethan always did say you were the most courageous one in the family.'

'He was right, you know. How sad that it took my father's death and his legacy to me to make me realise it myself. Believe what others had always seen in me. Had I blinded myself to the real Syrah for fear of offending Caleb? I did so want him to love me and Keoki, for being his sister and his nephew, part of the Richebourg clan. You'd better tell me the rest of it, James.'

'Caleb and Paula are now desperate because of those personal loans from Ira. They'd used their stock in Richebourg-Conti as collateral. They *must* have Ruy Blas and Ethan's wine cellar to save themselves and Richebourg-Conti. Richebourg's Ruy Blas is the most sought after and expensive wine produced in California. To obtain one case, a wine merchant must buy substantial amounts of Richebourg-Conti also. No hardship, mind you, because it is a first-class vintage. Both wines under one banner is what is wheeled and dealed for. Together they're the key to the Richebourg-Conti success. That's the way it's always been for as long as the wine men of the Napa Valley can remember.'

'I wonder if Caleb knows that Ira is trying to make a bid for my legacy? I can just hear them plotting: Caleb and Paula assuring Ira they will easily get Ruy Blas and the cellar because Syrah's not interested in working a vineyard. Though it will be an uphill battle to make the silly, extravagant woman see that her best option, for everyone's sake, is to sell it to them. Ira playing their game in the hope that it's true but believing that if he can effect a deal with me behind Paula and Caleb's back, he will then have the leverage to take over Richebourg-Conti. Oh, the sly bastard!'

'Now you see how vulnerable you are? It seems to be open season for shooting you down and a take over of the Richebourg wine dynasty. You do realise how desperate Caleb must be? He and Paula will try anything to take over Ruy Blas.'

'Save tell me the truth and ask me to help them,' she replied.

'I'll do everything I can to help you but there's no time left for procrastinating about what you're going to do. Whatever it is, you must take a grip and move quickly to leave Malibu and establish yourself at Ruy Blas. I believe with all my heart that Ethan thwarted Caleb and Paula and protected Richebourg-Conti by giving you power over his two greatest assets, Ruy Blas and the cellar.'

At last it was clear to Syrah why her father had left her such gifts. He had trusted her to keep them safe. She told James, 'I marvel that Ethan should have known me better than I do myself, that after his passing I would be drawn back to the Napa Valley he had taught me to love as a child. I can almost hear him, like a whisper on the wind saying, "The keys to a kingdom that is rightly yours and your son's."

'All I have to do is create my own kingdom out of my legacy. My own wine to rival Paula and Caleb's Richebourg-Conti. It's all there waiting for me and can be mine and Keoki's: fame, fortune, a new life for a penniless aristocrat of the wine world – if I have the will and the courage to fight to keep the privileges, the respected name, and follow in my father's footsteps. Even to become a Master of Wine as he was.'

'That's quite a lot to aspire to but I have no doubt that if anyone can do it, it will be you. There will be many friends in the Valley to help you out. Caleb and Paula have made enemies but Ethan remains close to people's hearts. They will do anything they can for him and his daughter. Even as we speak there are several men watching over Ruy Blas,' James told her.

Syrah rose from his lap and placed a tender kiss

upon his lips. As she walked round the table once more to take her place opposite him, she said with a tremor of nervousness in her voice, 'There's something more you have to tell me!'

The moment had come for James to tell Syrah just how bad things were at Ruy Blas. It pained him even to think that Caleb and Paula would behave in such a manner. But they were and Syrah had to know how rough things were getting. He found it difficult to look her in her eyes because he knew how the news would hurt her and could hardly bear to see her so pained.

'Caleb and Paula have hired thugs to vandalise Ruy Blas. They tried to wreck vineyard equipment, break down fences, have broken into and torched the small house on the vineyard, in an attempt to convince you what a burden the place is going to be for you. Henri Chagny, Bob Kidd and I caught two of the men in the act. Before we ran them off the vineyard, Bob made them confess who had hired them and why. We also learned that they'll be back. To quote one of them: "To finish the job a little bit at a time until Mr Richebourg calls us off." Ruy Blas now has a twenty-four-hour security system, armed men – old friends taking it on a rota, alarms and flood lights.'

'Did you call the police?' was all Syrah could think to say.

'Had the sheriff down. It seems we shouldn't have let the hired vandals go. Unless you want to press charges on Caleb there's not much the police can do now. Chevy

Brown and I went to school together, he's on our tribal council. He has no love for Caleb but works strictly by the book. Chevy's best suggestion was to try and settle it between you and Caleb before someone gets hurt. Until then he'll have a squad car run by Ruy Blas on their nightly cruises.'

'Caleb's playing dirty . . . that it should come to this! How they must hate me. How desperate they must be. I'll not press charges but I certainly will fight him off my land,' a despondent Syrah told James.

'You see why I can't stay the night with you? Something that I long to do. But I must get back to the Valley. I don't like being far from your vineyard with all that's going on. It will all be different once you're settled into the Valley. It's then we can think of ourselves. But first there's a great deal to settle, not only for you but for me as well.'

Syrah sensed a sadness in James, something deep and personal. He had obviously decided this was not the time or the place to discuss it with her. Not for the first time in the short while they'd been together Syrah sensed a certain hesitation in James. There was a shadow between them, but rather than confront whatever it was she trusted him enough to ignore it. She would wait for him to speak to her about that shadow, whenever and *if* ever he wanted to.

They rose from their chairs and walked into each other's arms to kiss. That seemed to strengthen them for whatever was to come. While they were still in a loving embrace, the phone began to ring. It went on for several rings before Syrah released herself from James to go and answer it. It was not for her but for James.

'Someone called Direnda Silverfeet for you.' And she handed the telephone over.

Syrah listened to the conversation but could glean little from it. She watched James, studied his handsome good looks, the proud bearing of pure American Indian blood that ran through his veins. The long dark hair, fine cheekbones, handsome sensuous lips. The long, slender, broad-shouldered body. She believed herself to be the luckiest woman in the world because he loved her.

James put down the telephone and turned to face Syrah. 'Direnda Silverfeet is a friend from childhood. Her family are wine people. She runs a wine magazine and is au fait with what's going on in the California wine world. She has just come from an interview with Caleb and Paula and thought I should know she is running a three-page story on their plans for the future of Richebourg-Conti. She wasn't for a minute fooled about why she had been offered the interview. Too much gossip about their losing Ruy Blas, the multi-million pound cellar also left to you, Ethan's death and what it would mean to Richebourg-Conti. Word of their debts and their desperate need to replant is out and its bad for business. Caleb and Paula no longer have time on their side so they gave the interview to detract from their problems by making public their expansion plans with Ira Rudman. Property development that will change the face of the Valley is big on their agenda, almost bigger than their plans to expand the vineyards of Richebourg-Conti.'

'What does that mean?' asked Syrah.

'A bigger fight to save the Valley, more people to fight off their expansion plans. Ira is a ruthless wheeler-dealer who has money and power, political friends in high places. But so have the wine people in the Valley. The newspapers are sure to pick it up before Direnda can get her magazine out but she wanted me to know immediately. She called Henri and he gave her your number. She'll be a great ally.'

Syrah wanted to drive James to the airport but he did not allow her to do that. 'I would rather you didn't. A public goodbye is more than I can handle.' She knew exactly what he meant for she had the same feelings about their parting. Instead she called for a taxi and followed it as it backed up her drive to turn into the main highway where it vanished amidst the evening traffic.

Now that Syrah's mind was made up about what she wanted to do vis-à-vis her legacy and her life, the first step was to talk to Keoki. It was after all his life at stake as well as hers. But unable to do that until the following day, she called Diana to tell her the news about the love that had blossomed between James and herself, her plans to leave Malibu as soon as possible. The two women were ecstatic about the changes Syrah was going to make in her life.

She made two other calls: one to her lawyer and the other to a friend who was a top real estate broker. Syrah told her the house must be sold as soon as possible. With the wheels set in motion she went to her room, took a long leisurely bath in almond-scented bath bubbles, then climbed into bed between the cream-coloured Pratesi sheets edged with ecru-coloured lace. Her last thought before she drifted into a deep, dreamless sleep was, What luxury! So long to such indulgences. Well, for the next few years anyway.

At eleven the following morning, Syrah was still asleep. Melba Morissey wakened her with a cup of tea, her favourite Earl Grey. She opened the curtains and the sun streamed into the bedroom.

'What time is it?' Syrah asked her housekeeper.

'You're going to be furious, it's eleven o'clock. I came in at eight and you were sleeping so soundly I left you to it. Keoki came in at ten and decided to let you sleep on. Now it's eleven and you've slept long enough. You must have been mighty tired, Syrah. You were asleep by the time I arrived last night to make your dinner.'

'Oh, so much has happened. Where is Keoki? I must talk with him.'

'He's down on the beach with the next-door neighbour's kids. Have some breakfast first. You can talk to him afterwards,' suggested Melba, who was as usual right.

An hour later, feeling fresh and with her energy high, Syrah looked through the messages Melba had taken. Mostly creditors dunning her for money. For the first time she no longer felt overwhelmed by the position she found herself in. She had set the wheels in motion, had a plan, knew at last where she was going and what she intended to do. Syrah put them aside and went down to the beach to find her son.

Keoki was just coming out of the ocean. On seeing his mother he broke away from the group of boys he had been swimming with and ran to join her, waving his arms above his head. Together mother and son walked along the nearly deserted beach, he playfully dashing in and out of the waves breaking on to the sand.

'Keoki, you are a clever boy. You must be aware that things are not as good as they were before Ethan died. No matter how I tried to shield you from what's going on, I sensed you understood my problems,' she bravely told her son.

'Our problems, Mom,' was his reply as he grasped her hand.

'Let me put it to you as simply as possible. There are only two options open to us. Either I sell our legacy and carry on living off that money in the style to which we are accustomed, or at least until the money runs out, which might be sooner than I'd hope because I have so many debts that have to be paid off. Or we sell everything we own, keep the legacy and I work the vineyard and the wine cellar. If we do the first nothing changes. If we do the second we will be vine and wine rich but cash poor and have to make many sacrifices in our lifestyle, work like demons and move to the vineyard. You must understand how really poor we will be when I have cleared our debts. The luxurious life we have been living will be over.

'Keoki, the last thing in this world I want to do is let you down. Give you less than you have always had. Tear you away from the fun and carefree life I have always been able to give you. But the real world has crashed in on us and we have to deal with it. That's why we're having this talk, you must have a say in what we do with our lives now.'

He squeezed his mother's hand, jumped up and gave her an affectionate peck on the cheek even as they were still walking. It was that little gesture that brought them to a halt. The tide was coming in and the water surging on to the sand covered their bare feet.

'Mom, what do *you* think we should do? What option do you think we should go for?' asked the boy.

Still holding hands, Syrah led her son away from the water's edge to sit on the dry hot sand. They faced the ocean and watched the tide roll in for several minutes before she cleared her throat and confided in her son.

'Keoki, Ethan's death and its consequences have had a profound effect on me. It has made me feel differently about the way we have been living. The legacy that he has left us was totally unexpected. It has presented us with a challenge, finding another way to live. It has given me something to work for, for us, in memory of his trust and generosity, his love for us.'

Syrah's voice began to quaver. Unconsciously she began wringing her hands. She felt herself breaking down but struggled on, 'I know I have been a good mother to you and that you love me, but I have let you down by not being more clever about work and money in the past. Now I have to sell our house, destroy our lifestyle, take you away from a school you love and your friends. I have decided to keep our legacy, work it, build on it for our future. I want to sell off everything here in Malibu, all our possessions, and move to the Valley, to live on the vineyard. But there is a way you can stay here and live, possibly more frugally. An alternative solution for you, darling, could be that you live with Diana in the week, and you and I could be together on weekends and your holidays.'

The boy was shocked by the suggestion. Tearful as much for his mother's anguish as for himself, he told her, 'Losing my grandfather will take me a long time to get over, but an arrangement where I might lose you for days on end . . . I might never get over that, Mom. No! We move to the vineyard together. I'll go to school and work on the vines in my spare time. I'll make new friends and bring my old ones up for holidays, and I can come back here and stay with them. We'll just shift gears, Mom. I'll think of it as an adventure. How many boys do you think there are who have their own vineyard *and* a mom with her own plane? The plane! Can we save your plane or must that go too?'

'No, that's about all we will be able to salvage. We'll have to make it work for us, rent it out or compete at air shows with it. Who knows? Even join a flying circus.'

'You see, life won't be so bad for us, Mom!'

Chapter 9

Melba had been watching Syrah and Keoki when they walked together down the beach. Syrah need not have said anything; her behaviour at breakfast had been more positive than it had been since Ethan's demise. Her body language said it all. The moment of truth had come and she was facing it and confiding in her son.

Melba knew she was next to be told how bad things were for Syrah and what she had decided to do about it. Melba did, of course, know most of it already. The creditors and that horrible visit from Caleb, the way Syrah was treated by her brother and sister-in-law, left little to the imagination. She would have had to be deaf and blind not to hear and see what was going on. And there was the legacy, Syrah had told her about that. There were in fact few things that employer and employee did not confide in each other. That was the way of their relationship.

In the kitchen the housekeeper decided on spare ribs and rice with lots of cooked greens, Keoki's favourite. She looked at her wristwatch and started the meal. The boy was always ravenous by half-past twelve and Melba was meticulous about timing. The scent of barbecued spare ribs filled the house. On hearing Syrah and Keoki bounding up the stairs that led from the beach to their sun deck, she dropped the spring greens into boiling salted water just long enough for mother and son to get to the kitchen and the greens to be blanched.

Keoki and Syrah arrived just as the platter of ribs was being placed on the table. 'Right on time but what glum-looking faces,' she declared.

'Smells terrific, my favourite!' said Keoki.

Syrah marvelled at how quickly children bounce back from traumatic events. 'We have to talk, Melba,' she told her housekeeper.

'Not until dessert. I'm not having my meal ruined,' she answered cheekily.

The pudding, home-made cherry ice cream, was duly served. The attempt to keep cheerful for the meal was now abandoned. Syrah said, 'Keoki, would you mind having ice cream somewhere else? I'd like to explain everything to Melba.'

The boy rose from his chair and went around to Melba to give her a kiss on the cheek. 'You can't fool me, you made me my favourite meal because you thought I needed something to take away the sting Mom has just delivered. Listen, you two, I'm no baby, I can roll with the punches.' And he walked away, spooning ice cream into his mouth.

Syrah saw no need to hide any of the facts of what was happening in her life and explained everything in detail: how her income had been cut off by Caleb, the rift between them, her legacy, that she was debt-ridden and unable to maintain the lifestyle they had all enjoyed so much and naively thought would go on forever. That it was over.

'Melba, I'm poor, without money and unable to raise any to live off. We have been living from hand to mouth since my father's death. I am so flat broke I can't even afford to keep you on. You will have to find another position,' Syrah told her housekeeper, then burst into sobs.

Appalled, Melba sat silently, not knowing what to say. Finally she went to a kitchen drawer and drew from it a white linen napkin. She handed it to Syrah with the comment, 'Best wipe up those tears, Syrah, they'll get us nowhere.'

The housekeeper pulled her chair closer. 'Oh, stop it, girl! I know these are terrible times for you – that's the way of this cruel world and there's not much you can do about it except give survival the best shot you can. OK, you made your decisions, you're being courageous. But, girl, you got to take account of the fact you know nothing of what it is to work, to be rock bottom poor and looking for where your next meal is coming from. We sure do know you're ignorant about money, know nothing about business, and most of all what your life would be like without Melba to care for you and Keoki,' she told Syrah, the blunt reality of her words brought tears to her own eyes and stained her cheeks. The two women hugged each other for comfort.

Melba wiped the tears from her face with the back of

her hand before she spoke. 'Believe me, I know about destitute. That was where I was when you took in me and my fifteen-year-old son, gave me a job and us both a home. I'm going nowhere and certainly not looking for another job. We'll weather this disaster together. Make no mistake, you'll need me more than ever now you're going to be a working mother.'

'But there's no money to pay your wages, Melba,' protested Syrah, by then wracked with guilt that she should have to turn her housekeeper out.

'Money doesn't come into it, Syrah. We can settle when you have it, and have it I am certain you will. God will favour you, he always has. No! Don't argue. Remember, Syrah, money didn't come into it when you put my son through university and graduate school. No more protests, please. I'll be moving with you from our old Malibu life to our new Napa Valley life. And that's final.'

The next few weeks were a horrifying experience for Syrah who was unused to the grim reality of having to sell off her possessions, and have the banks grab every penny from her assets to reduce her loans and mortgage; having to account to the tax man for her every financial move also. Not able to bear to put Keoki through the trauma of seeing their home vanishing, piece by piece, to greedy dealers she had naively thought to be friends, she begged him to stay at Diana's house until they were ready to move to the vineyard. Her paintings, all contemporary and by big names in the international art world, were bought for a fraction of their true worth. Her many so-called friends, knowing her situation, drove hard bargains for her possessions. More sensitive friends vanished overnight the moment her hard times became public.

At night, alone in her bed, she was sustained by love for her dead father and the very much alive James whom she was certain was shaping a new life for himself, as she was working on her own, so they might come together as the lovers they were meant to be. James's phone calls gave her courage to wait for him to claim her for his own on a more permanent basis than love and friendship from afar. They hardened her to do all she must to win through to a new life.

None of what was happening was easy. Everything seemed more traumatic than she'd expected. It hurt more than Syrah had ever imagined it would, this disposal of a life that had been such a happy one for her and Keoki. She was selling off pieces of their life, not mere possessions. It was depressing and somehow frightening to be stripped down to a nakedness of the heart and soul, of life itself. She had never envisaged how ugly it could get, how cruel people could be in the name of debt, money, the demon power. There were times when she felt she was drowning, being sucked down into murky water. But through it all there was Ruy Blas, a beacon to swim towards.

The stress was almost unbearable but she bore it with fortitude, only worrying about Keoki and how much he was suffering from the move. On the surface he appeared to be handling things better than his mother. But was he? She spoke often to James about it and because Syrah was so concerned, he decided to fly down for a day to have lunch at Diana's where Syrah, Melba and Keoki were now staying, the Malibu house having been sold. Syrah saw her son's face light up when she told him, 'James is coming for lunch to tell us what it will be like living in the Napa Valley.'

Willoughby was never happier than when Keoki and Syrah were staying with Diana. The house seemed to come alive, was filled with laughter and good times. Having Melba as a guest was an extra bonus, a challenge for him. The two housekeepers were always trying to outdo one another with their hospitality, great cooking and brilliant organisation. But the Richebourg household on this particular visit was downright glum and it was hard work to please any of them. They had been there for nearly two weeks when Diana announced that a visitor was flying down for lunch. For the first time their spirits seemed to lift. Keoki talked to Willoughby about James Whitehawk, said that he was a Californian Indian, how great he'd been to Keoki at the funeral.

Syrah listened to her son. Though she'd known when Keoki and James had met that they had taken to each other, she had not realised how much her son had liked James. It raised her spirits, and that was picked up by Diana and Melba.

It was all so easy, so right, the way James slipped

instantly into Syrah's life that day. He had an immediate rapport with both Diana and Melba, and as for Keoki, he was the son James had never had, a part of the woman he had always loved. He already loved the boy as his own.

Lunch was served by the pool and so it was there that they all sat round drinking long cool drinks before they were called to the table. James was clearly besotted with Syrah, could hardly keep his eyes off her for a minute. It was the warmth and charm he exuded towards them without trying to win them over that endeared him to them. Diana saw him as a part of their lives forever. Keoki was slightly in awe of him as a grown man and new friend. Melba simply saw him as something more than any man Syrah had ever got involved with before.

'Tell us what it's like to live in the Valley, James? I know the place, of course. I was after all born there. But I never lived there except on weekends and holidays sometimes. I was always there for Christmas dinner, but that's not living there, is it? I'm thinking of it as a big adventure. It is an adventure, isn't it?' asked Keoki.

'I think that's a good way to think of life in the Napa Valley. It's my home, has been my family's home for hundreds of years, your family, too, have been there for many generations, so I think you will take to it. It will be like coming home once you have settled in. I really came down to give you all a more comprehensive picture of the Napa Valley wine world with its hard work, competitiveness, passion for the grape and the land, the politics of wine and the skulduggery that is sometimes practised in the trade. You have to know about those things because that's life in the Valley.'

'How fascinating. I grew up with that sort of life going on all round me and have forgotten so much of it. It seems that yet again I'm jumping in at the deep end, unprepared for the job ahead of me,' commented Syrah.

'Maybe unprepared but you'll learn fast. Word is out that you are moving into Ruy Blas and plan to work your vineyard. It would be good for you all to remember that you have ready-made friends awaiting your arrival in the Valley. Just like me, they're committed to helping you in any way they can. They are other small vineyard owners, real wine men, disenchanted with Caleb and Paula who have been going up against them with Ira Rudman. Trying to buy them out at a fraction of their vineyards' true value during these hard times.'

Keoki, standing next to James's chair, listened attentively to every word he uttered. The boy looked troubled. James reached for his hand and pulled him down to sit next to him. Keoki leaned against James who placed an arm round his shoulders.

'Don't look so troubled. I know your mom, she's a Richebourg, cut from the same cloth as her father. She'll go up against Paula and Caleb with the other vineyard owners who are fighting to save the Napa Valley for wine. And you both have me.'

'Why are the vineyards having such a hard time?' asked Diana.

'Vineyards work on the edge. They're always at the

mercy of the elements and of root disease which has hit the Napa Valley very badly for the last few years. Then they have to go up against the Ira Rudmans of this world who are buying every parcel of land in the Valley for development that is sure to ruin the area. Vital, rich land that the small growers need for expansion is being sacrificed to greed. They have no chance to save themselves because Ira can pay more, wheel and deal with authorities and investors. He wants to turn the valley into hotels and condos. Buy a great winery for his ego and achieve international acclaim in the wine world. He is a dilettante who wants to buy a wine dynasty, a gentleman's business, and remove himself from the stigma of being a ruthless tenement landlord. Syrah has said no to Caleb and Paula. No to Ira. But Ira will not give up, so be warned.'

None of this was easy for Diana to hear. She had been cushioned by her passion for Ira and had never listened to what people had said about him. Now it was over for them, she no longer felt the pain of losing the man she had once loved beyond measure, but she was yet again appalled by Ira's tactics and greed. How the man had been swallowed up by those things he was obsessed with and his lust for personal power.

'Ira is a ruthless predator whom we must all approach with caution,' James warned. 'The only thing that will save all our small, prestigious, vineyards is if wine people, not realtors, back each other till the vineyards revive from the crippling root disease and reach a gentleman's agreement against selling out to Ira Rudman or any others like Richebourg-Conti who are in cahoots with him.'

Keoki, still snuggled against James, listened intently and commented, 'It doesn't sound dull in the Napa Valley. And my mom is going to be in the middle of this?'

'I sure am!' replied Syrah, a twinkle of excitement in her eyes.

Keoki sat up and looked at James. 'My mom always rises to a challenge, you should see her in an air show,' he said proudly.

Everyone laughed. All of them could attest to that. How could they have forgotten what Syrah could be like? Her courage and bravado. Too many disasters falling upon her one after the other, her sudden aloneness had made them forget who and what she was in herself. How strong a woman she could be, and would be in adversity. A nine-year-old boy had jolted those sitting round his mother into the realisation that they were all about to follow Syrah once again into an adventure. To her boy in his innocence the collapse of the world he lived in was an adventure, not destitution.

'Oh, darling,' Syrah said, with a look of pride and love for her son.

It was a touching moment. Syrah broke the spell when she announced, 'We simply have to go up against Ira.'

'That takes money, a great deal of money,' cautioned James.

'I have a great deal of money and I'd like to invest it,' said Diana. 'I'll bankroll the vineyards in trouble with an investment of $4.5 million. You will be able to challenge Ira for as long as my money holds out on condition that I remain a silent and very secret investor. As long as the vineyard owners agree to put up their vineyards and wine as security, and they and my investment consultants can come to an agreement on advantageous interest rates and a time scale, I see no problem.'

Turning to Syrah, she said, 'That, of course, includes what is needed at Ruy Blas. But I want to make one thing clear. The object of this investment is to keep the Napa Valley for wine instead of a tourist haven that Ira or anyone else might capitalise on.'

The group were stunned into silence by Diana's suggestion. Overwhelmed to have the famous actress as their patron. Syrah sensed that Diana might be making this offer as a means of revenge on Ira. But there was no way Syrah could allow her to chance her money if that was the purpose behind the gesture placed so generously before them. She rose from her chair and, taking Diana's hand, pulled her up. 'Will you all excuse us for a few minutes?' she asked as the two women walked from the pool to the gardens.

'You're not doing this as some sort of revenge on Ira, for being the bastard he has been? If that's the reason, I can't allow you to gamble your life's savings, it simply isn't worth it,' said Syrah.

Diana laughed then told her, 'I admit I would like to thwart Ira's dream just once but that's different from revenge. Revenge it might have been had I still wanted a life with him. That's no longer the case. My love for Ira is gone and nothing can revive it. It's all quite straightforward: I want to save the Valley from him. I will fight in any way I can to see that he falls flat on his face in this bid to take over the small independent vineyards. I'm doing it for them, for you and Keoki, for me, maybe even for Ethan. Remember I come from poor mountain farming people who had to beat off the banks and the land developers all their working lives. It's quite simple, Ira doesn't deserve to be a force in the Napa Valley. Or maybe, put even more simply, I don't want him to be.'

The two women hugged each other and then, arm in arm, walked back to James and shook his hand. 'Allies in a quest,' said Syrah.

'I don't know what to say. This is so unexpected, so marvellous for all concerned,' replied an overwhelmed James.

'And it means so much to me. Frankly I was daunted by all I have to do and concerned about going it alone. But now with your support, Diana, and knowing I will be accepted and helped by the other vineyards in the Valley, I will learn my new trade as I work my vineyard and my cellar. I will settle for nothing less than producing the best Richebourg-Ruy Blas yet.'

'Now *that's* what we need to hear,' commented Melba, and everyone gave Syrah a standing ovation and burst into laughter, released from a dark place into the light.

Willoughby's timing was perfect. It was then that he

announced lunch was served. It was a joyful occasion. The first course was fresh asparagus with a light hollandaise sauce.

Syrah warned, 'Keoki, I don't see asparagus on our table for a long time after this meal.'

When the main course came, stuffed roasted quail and game chips with a compôte of fresh cranberries, she said, 'We'll be lucky to have pasta to eat, quail will seem like a dream. In fact, all our life here in Southern California will be like a glorious dream compared to the hard working life ahead of us.'

When the pudding was served she began again. It was a gorgeous Baked Alaska with a Cherry Jubilee sauce poured over it. 'How divinely extravagant! Eat your fill, Keoki, because I don't see many meals like this in our future.'

'Stop! Just stop there, Syrah,' said James, but with a twinkle in his eye.

Turning to Keoki, he said, 'Your mom is so busy mourning the loss of Baked Alaska in her life she's forgotten to tell you what living on Ruy Blas and in the Napa Valley will be like. Oh, yes, you will miss all the things you grew up with here: the Pacific Ocean rolling up to your front door, living on a grand scale, your friends and school. Melba's cooking with extravagant produce may change to beans on toast but, hey, she'll make them taste like filet mignon. Turn sardines into smoked salmon.'

Everyone laughed and that included Syrah who said,

'I can't believe I said those things! Imagine mourning the loss of a Baked Alaska after what I have been going through.' And she raised her glass and made a toast, 'To my son, and what lies before us in the Valley.'

Chapter 10

In the weeks that had passed since James had fallen in love with Syrah at the graveside at Ethan's funeral, and later boldly taken her in his arms in the garden, he had come to realise that a mere seduction of her would not be enough for either one of them. Sex, love and friendship would govern the affair that neither one of them would ever break. They were, right from the beginning in the garden of the château, embroiled in a serious involvement which meant they would have to live double lives, something he was loath to demand from her.

It was for that reason that, once Syrah had returned to Malibu, he made a supreme and conscious effort to spend more constructive and loving time with his wife. It took no effort to be with the children whom he loved. Betsy and Carrie were the only reason he remained with his wife. The marriage had been going wrong for them for years but it was bearable so long as he had not fallen in love elsewhere.

James tried, those first weeks after falling in love with Syrah, to control his ardour for her. He cultivated several

163

sexual encounters in his quest to dampen the fire burning within him for her. It worked . . . but only for a few days. After each fling Syrah was back in his mind and his heart. James was more lonely, more hungry than ever to be with her. To have her always in his life.

Now that Syrah was moving to the valley to run Ruy Blas, she would be closer to him and his world. That both thrilled and frightened him. He knew under those new circumstances he would be unable to resist his desire for her. Before the lunch at Diana's house he had thought he would bide his time. Maybe their love would fade enough for them to live with it and do nothing about it. He had thought that they would both be able, for a while, to live a clandestine life together because there were two families at stake and greater pressures than love to deal with. But of course he was wrong. Their love and lust for each other was too good, too right, to be conducted as a cheap backstreet romance.

Now here he was waiting at a private airfield several miles from Ruy Blas for Syrah, Keoki and Melba to circle the field in her tangerine Boeing Stearman and he had yet to sit down and tell her about the state of his marriage and his love for his two daughters which governed everything in his life. He loved Syrah the more for never having asked about them and wondered if she even knew they existed. Trust. It was all a matter of trust. She trusted him to tell her about his personal life, any commitments he might have, when it was the right time to do so and not before. Every day he had talked to her on the telephone he had asked the same question, 'Is this the right time?'

He saw a flash of colour in the bright blue sky, a sun beam on the tangerine double-winged plane, and once more he asked himself, Is it now? Has the moment come to confess all to the woman I love?

The plane landed and it was high excitement that greeted James and the airfield's owner, Jake Blackwolf, who had agreed to allow Syrah the run of the grass airfield that ran down the centre of his vineyard. Jake was one of the small growers committed to helping her get on her feet in the wine trade.

'Welcome to the Valley, Miss Syrah. You keep your plane here as long as you like. It's a lot rougher field than the one your daddy made for you at Richebourg-Conti but no matter, you'll get used to it, and I'm proud to have Ethan's girl using it,' he told her while shaking her hand.

They settled the plane next to Jake's Leopard Moth in a shabby but adequate hangar and all piled into James's Range Rover to set off for Ruy Blas. Melba could hardly keep her eyes off Jake Blackwolf who was, like James, a full-blooded Native American whose forefathers had always been chiefs of the Yurok tribe. He was tanned and lean, his white hair worn long and tied back in a pony tail. There was something noble in his bearing. He made Melba stand a little taller, raise her chin a little higher. Jake emanated a power that quietly took you over. Having met him, Melba for the first time truly understood that she, Syrah and Keoki were returning to the earth, to a real world inhabited by real people with whom they had nothing in common. She felt humbled by this stranger as well as safe with men like him and James. In this luscious valley of many vineyards, she felt more of a pioneer than a stranger, one who might have crossed the great plains a hundred or so years ago discovering the grass roots of America.

To feel like that on landing was one thing but once they drove through the ancient iron gates emblazoned 'Ruy Blas' and guarded by a blond young man with a rifle slung over his shoulder, who tipped his Stetson to James and Syrah, she realised that settling into this life was going to be more of a struggle than she had expected it to be. The house was little more than a shack and had been damaged by the fire Caleb's men had set yet everything else, particularly the row upon row of vines, was pristine, kept in perfect order and magnificent condition. It didn't take long for the three from Malibu to realise they were now living in a working vineyard where vines came first and humans second.

Each of them put on a good face for the others and took their new life one day at a time. There were more people working on the Ruy Blas vineyard than Syrah had realised. She was impressed by Henri and the dedication he and the staff showed to the vineyard as well as how helpful they were to her, Keoki and Melba. But after no more than a week Syrah felt the pressure of money being so scarce and the people, though kind, incredibly provincial. She did not find it unpleasant exactly, merely difficult to get used to.

Almost every day James was there to give them all support and for the first time Syrah and he had time to be alone together. Syrah bathed in the light of James's affection for her. Every day their kisses and caresses took on a new intimacy that turned their world into something more heavenly than earth-bound. So many times during a day their need to consummate their lust for one another became too strong to resist and sexual fantasies seemed always on the brink of being fulfilled. Unable to resist, their sex life was conducted in thrilling episodes: in a wood on a sunny day, naked in a cove with the Pacific Ocean crashing over them, one night at dusk among the vines. And every day James thought he must tell Syrah he could not marry her.

He had been waiting for the right moment, the right time and place, to talk to her about his plight. And then one day while he was making love to her, when they were both on the edge of coming together in a long and exquisite orgasm, he knew there would never be a right time. They came and the orgasm was so intense, the experience so overwhelmingly thrilling, that James knew nothing in the world could ever take away what they had together. Nothing but a reluctant decision to part.

He slid off her body and held her in his arms as she went down on him and licked his penis. She wanted not to waste a drop of his lust. He felt the same way about Syrah and was thrilled when she came twice more as he lingered over her cunt with his tongue and lips. Then he inched his way up her body and cradled her in his arms.

He spoke softly but clearly. 'My wife's name is Katherine and I will never leave her because I love my children. In the past I have tried to leave her, but she will never allow me to. You see, she blackmails me with threats of destroying my daughters' love for me. Indeed, destroying their lives if necessary.'

James could see the shocked expression on Syrah's face. 'Oh, my dear, you do want to marry me then?'

'With all my heart and soul,' he replied.

'Then what are you saying, James? Or, to put it more bluntly, what are you asking me? That I must make the decision to be your mistress and nothing more?' asked Syrah.

'You must think about this, my dearest heart. Until you make that decision I would like us to agree to go on seeing each other as we have been but to try to cool our ardour. I feel it only fair that I should spend some time with my wife and the girls, and you, Syrah, should try and find a man who can marry you and give you what you so richly deserve: a husband of your own to pamper, love and adore you.'

Syrah was aware that there was little she could do about their situation. It was all up to James. If he could not bear for her to live in a clandestine relationship, it was no easier for her to put any pressure on him and force him to take a drastic step that might harm his children. She truly loved James. So much so that it was not at all painful for her to stay with him in any way that she could, seeing him how and when that was possible. Finally they agreed to be discreet but not secretive about being together.

And so they saw each other at the vineyard and on outings where they could enjoy each other and make love. Only the pain of separation each time they parted haunted their every meeting, their every kiss. For Syrah that pain was sharp and short-lived because in her heart she felt certain James was her man, that they were destined to love no other. He was hers. She had even come to accept that they might possibly have other husbands, other wives, but they would never leave each other or love another in the same way. At James's insistence, though, Syrah was determined at least to look for another man so as not to be a burden on James and the love they were able to share.

The joy of her life those first few weeks at Ruy Blas was first and foremost walking through her vineyard: she enjoyed seeing the row upon row of vines with their luscious array of bright green leaves and tight sensual clusters of grapes, the scent of the fruit, feeling underfoot the earth, the hot sun above as it beat down and ripened her crop. The winery that Ethan had installed for Ruy Blas became a second home for her, the place where she studied methods of blending, saw for herself the care with which her grapes were treated in every process they went through. There was so much to learn and James, Henri and the other workers admired her enthusiasm to master it all. She worked from dawn to dusk, either on the land, in the winery or in Ethan's cellar where she was beginning to appreciate the magnificent vintages. It calmed her to think of them as better than money in the bank; excited her to see herself as an important vineyard owner with a cellar that was sure to save Ruy Blas if bad times hit it. The more she worked and learned, the more Syrah wanted to push forward. Before long she had made up her mind to begin the studies that would eventually lead to her taking stringent exams to become a Master of Wine just as Ethan had been and as James was.

And so her days were filled with work, finding ways to make ends meet and loving James. She had never been happier except possibly when Keoki had been born. If Syrah was disconcerted about anything it was what was going on at Richebourg-Conti. It was only just surviving on its stocks and managing the outstanding bank loans with enormous difficulty. Because the banks were unhappy about the loss of Ruy Blas and Ethan's cellar they had even threatened foreclosure on Richebourg-Conti unless something drastic was done to inject money into the vineyard and its winery.

Caleb and Paula, under severe pressure, lost all sense of decency and mounted a renewed attack on Syrah. Before she could even approach the banks to raise money for her vineyard, Caleb advised them of her ignorance of the wine industry and said she should be considered a bad risk. Syrah was dependent on credit from the merchants who dealt in supplies for the wine industry. There were few who ignored Caleb's warning to them that giving her credit would be foolhardy and seen as an offence against Richebourg-Conti, bad enough for Caleb and Paula to withdraw any custom they were at present giving the traders.

Not for a day did her brother and sister-in-law stop harassing her with endless demands for machinery and barrels they claimed were owned by them and only loaned to Ruy Blas. Such demands cost Syrah time and trouble and constant litigation which she could not afford. They hired bullies to stalk and taunt her, Keoki, even Melba, and created a dozen small problems merely to waste her time: a lorry load of fertiliser dropped on the road to the house from the vineyard, earth moved and piled up in the entrance to the caves that had been converted into Ethan's wine cellar; the worst was a herd of sheep let loose among the vines.

Constant harassment was making Syrah's life a misery, her struggle harder. Yet fearful as she was for herself and her child, and for the vineyard which she now had guarded twenty-four hours a day against sabotage, she continued to throw herself headlong into learning about her chosen trade. Her reward was that every day she found herself happier than she had ever dreamed she could be.

Only after working at Ruy Blas for nearly a month did she begin to understand what a valuable gift Ethan had left her. She worked incessantly on valuing her wine collection and deciding how to market it, but first and foremost was the commitment she had made to study wine with the Association of Masters of Wine. She travelled from vineyard to vineyard in California and abroad to learn from friendly owners every aspect of wine making so she could produce the finest wine

Ruy Blas could possibly yield.

Keoki settled in better than anyone had expected he would and became the pride of Ruy Blas. He loved the vineyards and was as eager to learn about and be a part of them as his mother was. He spent a great deal of time with James, especially when Syrah was away earning money to keep the vineyard going. After conferring with James, her old friend Diego Juarez and Henry Hawthorne Halliwell, all wine men sympathetic to what she was doing, on their advice Syrah sold only enough rare wine from her cellar to give her half what she needed to keep going. The other half she decided she would earn by flying. They all agreed that the cellar was her most valuable asset and should be depleted as little as possible.

Diego and Henry had flown to Ruy Blas to see the cellar and its contents and there they saw a side of Syrah they'd never dreamed existed. The sacrifices that she and her son were making to work the vineyard impressed them beyond measure. They offered any support she might need, no little thing. These were big men in the wine world. Henry was a world-famous connoisseur of fine wine, a collector and Master of Wine. He was a prominent New York socialite, old money but with a new ethic of achievement. For many years he and Syrah had been friends, playboy and playgirl together. Beguiled by her latest manifestation, and fascinated by her struggles to make a success of her vineyard on her terms and in her way, he willingly became her client and bought the wine it was necessary for her to sell. Overnight the world learned that Syrah Richebourg had, and was trading, one of the most extraordinary cellars of fine wine. Within weeks enquiries were flooding in. She was the new and sought after wine name, her fame even extending to the Internet.

At that stage Syrah could have solved her financial worries at a stroke but she refused to sell one more bottle of rare wine from Ethan's collection. The French and English collectors, and particularly the auction houses, wished to view the caves if nothing else. She was incredibly polite, business-like and firm, putting them all off. Instead she went to see her flying friends and was quite candid with them.

Ben Canfield had taught Syrah to fly. He considered her one of the best women pilots and knew she was always a star attraction at the air shows he organised all round the world. For years she had flown with him and their friends purely for love. It was therefore a surprise to him and his partner, Ed Sweeney, when she flew into their base near Los Angeles to ask for paid work.

After an ecstatic welcome and a surprise lunch Ben had organised with some of her other flying friends, thoroughly relaxed and happy to be back in this part of her old life, Syrah began telling them about her new existence in the Napa Valley and her vineyard. These were very close friends whom she had known for years. It was easy to tell them about her financial problems with Ruy Blas, the cellar and her intention to work it and make something of herself in the wine world. No one seemed surprised. Rumours had abounded and most of the men at the table who had known and liked Ethan had flown up to the funeral to give her moral support and pay their last respects. They understood what a devastating loss Syrah had suffered with the death of her father.

She looked round the table and said, 'I need to earn money, as much and as fast as I can. Charity flying is over for me. Charity must now start at home. I want to fly for money: crop dusting, air shows, working county fairs where I can take people up for rides, air taxi piloting for wealthy businessmen and women, stunt flying, long-distance races here or abroad. All the money I earn will be put back into Ruy Blas and wine.'

This world of vintage aircraft and collectors was a relatively small one where everyone knew everyone else because of their mutual passion for flying and collecting handsome aircraft. After lunch the men retreated to Ben's office and sat round over a bottle of champagne discussing who would call whom to announce Syrah's availability. They called Diego in Chile first who immediately told them he would host a rally there. Vic Norman and Nick Mason spoke to them from their restored First World War airfield in Gloucestershire, England. They were enthusiastic about Syrah's entering the commercial side of vintage flying, offering to include her in several races that were being organised and to keep her informed about the many other events in England, Italy and France.

All the old excitement of flying returned to Syrah then. To be once again among those who loved aviation and its challenges, prizing vintage aircraft like jewels from another age; men and women who were courageous and daring, who flew always that little bit faster, higher, played with their aircraft and space like dancers on the top of their form, seemed so right for Syrah.

Almost immediately she had work in the air as well as on the ground and, amazingly, was able to schedule her time in such a manner that nothing suffered. She was leading the life she was determined to have and winning through. In her work and her travels Syrah was meeting attractive men. She made an effort with them, hoping she could find a man to love more than James even though he and Syrah were still together every chance that came their way. They never spoke of his wife nor of the several men who were pursuing Syrah.

One such admirer approached her when she was visiting a cooperage to buy much-needed oak barrels for her wine. She had met Sam Holbrook at her father's funeral and a spark had flared but quickly died between them. She had, however, felt he would always be a friend. But now, in his office, Syrah saw him again as a sensual man, undoubtedly attractive, someone she might be able to become interested in. They conducted their business and he invited her to dinner. She was not surprised; Syrah could always sense when a man wanted her.

For several weeks Sam and Syrah enjoyed a discreet but open affair. They freely acknowledged who and what they were, which strengthened their friendship but ultimately ended the relationship.

What Sam inevitably had to say came one night at a restaurant. It was a shock to her that he should choose a public place for such an intimate conversation, that he should even say what he did.

'There are things that have to be said, Syrah,' he began, a coldness in his voice she had never heard before.

'Yes,' was all she could manage in reply.

'I think we both know that I am falling in love with you – something more, I think, than either of us expected. It's never been a secret, your love for James. After all, I have seen you both together. One of us has to face the fact that you're only going through the motions of an affair of the heart with me. It is sexually satisfying but can go nowhere because you love someone else. I think we're both too honest to carry on with this any longer, don't you?'

Syrah felt as if she had been slapped in the face with a velvet glove. Facing the truth brought tears to her eyes but she managed to hold them there. By force of will she made them vanish. She was, however, choked with emotion and so remained silent.

Sam continued, 'I think it best for the three of us that you and I give up seeing each other in such an intimate way in favour of friendship. In this way no one cheats anyone and no one will be hurt.'

With that he raised his glass and toasted her. 'Goodbye, my love. Hello, my friend.'

Syrah drained her champagne flute dry before going round the table to Sam who rose from his chair. She kissed him gently on the lips and told him, 'You will understand if I don't stay for dinner?'

'Is it necessary for you to go?' he asked.

'Very. You've given me a great deal to think about, and of course you're right about us. I will always remember what a good friend you are.' Then she turned on her heel and walked from the restaurant.

While driving back from San Francisco to the Valley, Syrah could only think of how dishonest she had been with Sam. How right he had been to dump her and make her face up to what she was doing with other men. Everyone but James.

She kept thinking about men. How fearful she was of one taking over her and her son's life. How wrapped up she now was in the survival of her vineyard, too much so to think about any life other than the one she was struggling through. Her thoughts turned to her love for James and she realised that the impermanent basis of it would simply have to be enough. Whereas sex and love, with him were a priority, marriage was not. That was, and had to be, right for them both.

'What a waste of energy, this going out with other men. No more of it!' She could not imagine why she and James had thought she should be free to find someone who could give her more than he was able to do. All her energy in any case had been directed toward the survival of the vineyard and winery, in caring for and nurturing Keoki and loving James. This was her life and no other could take precedence. It was at that moment that she gave up any thought of another man and happily settled for true love with James, in whatever form it came.

It had been with only half a heart that she'd dated and bedded these other suitors. She'd never been happy about what she was doing, had made every effort to stop herself from thinking of anything other than sex for the sake of erotic fulfilment, sex of the sort she had had before James had come back into her life. She and her partners had been adventurous, had fucked on the edge of depravity to know the thrill of heightened sex and orgasm. And the truth of the matter was that it *was* thrilling to reach such peaks of sexual bliss when in the throes of lust, but she came to think of it in time as mere masturbation, not loving sex within a relationship. She would stop now. Syrah was simply too much in love and lust with James, and much as she had wanted to relieve herself of the burden of her love for him, she could not cheat either him or herself of what they had together.

The next day Syrah climbed into her rusty old pick-up lorry and drove across from her vineyard to James's. She waved to the workers in both vineyards because by know she was known and admired and a constant visitor to Whitehawk Ridge. She was relieved to see his Range Rover there for she had been so anxious to see James she hadn't even bothered to call. He was just coming out of the winery as she drove up to its doors.

Syrah leaped from the lorry and ran into his arms. They kissed and he slid an arm around her waist. His face lit up with the joy of her being there, as it always did every time they met. Then someone in a car with a trailer attached honked the horn and waved at them. They waved back. James and Syrah were an item locally and made no secret of their love affair. They were only secretive or discreet when there was a possibility that Katherine, his wife, was liable to see them.

'Great surprise, I didn't expect to see you today. I thought you were away,' said James.

'I *am* away, flying for a family's birthday treat. Come with me, please? It's only a few hours' work. Can you get away?' she asked.

'Will you be back in time for lunch?'

'Yes,' she replied, and gave a sigh of relief that they were to be together.

'I'll pick you up at Blackwolf's hangar at one o'clock,' he told her and Syrah smiled and kissed him on the cheek before she dashed back to her lorry.

James took her to a small Mexican restaurant in the hills, one of their favourite places, where they took rooms and ordered a meal which would be served on the terrace of their suite. The place was famous for its food and its air of intimacy. The owner played the guitar and his brother the cornet, soft and lazy tunes filled with nostalgia for Old Mexico, romance, love and tenderness. Afterwards they sat in the sun, Syrah leaning against James, both drinking Tequila Gimlets.

'I love you, Syrah,' he told her.

'I know, and I love you. That's why I wanted to see

you so much today,' she told him and sat up and away from him.

'Is something wrong?' he asked.

'Oh, no. It's more that something is so right. James, I have something to tell you. I can no longer waste my time going out with other men and sleeping with them in the hope of distancing myself from you. I truly don't want my love to be a burden on you and your family but I have fucked without love, for the sake of fun, all my life until I met you again. There seemed nothing wrong in that at the time. I had no commitments, no relationship that was deep and loving, and nor did my partners. But I can't do that anymore.

'I love you, I'm committed to you, no matter how you want to label that commitment, and to fuck a stranger I'm indifferent to is to make myself a whore and a cheat. I am not and never have been that sort of woman. I took the wrong road trying to spare you, I'll not do that again. I can accept being your mistress for all to see and behave discreetly as one. You'll have to learn to live with that if I can.'

'I thought I was trying to spare you the indignity of being a mistress,' he protested. 'But maybe I was just being weaker than you are about facing up to what we are together. Forgive me. What a fool I've been,' James told her, and pulled her once more into his arms.

The lunch arrived and they watched a young Mexican girl lay the table: a white cotton cloth embroidered with white silk flowers; terracotta pottery dishes and bowls of glazed brightly coloured flowers; silver flatware and goblets of blue glass. Dishes of beans and rice, tacos, enchiladas and chicken cooked in a chocolate sauce. A jug of chilled red wine. The proprietor's wife arrived to serve the lovers and the sound of a guitar and cornet wafted upwards. Once served, James and Syrah were left to dine alone.

Some invisible barrier that had remained between them vanished then. Never had either of them felt so intimately involved with another soul. They had known months ago that they were as one but that afternoon they were *being*, not just knowing.

At first there was something tentative in their love making. Such tenderness only heightened their orgasms. They wallowed in their love of sex with each other; caressed and licked and sucked each other as if they were a feast tasted for the very first time. They lay in each other's arms, naked and wound together for eternity, and spoke from their hearts and souls. Then gradually they left tenderness behind because passion and lust were driving them to desire for further, more thrilling orgasms. They left their egos and their hearts in limbo for a time so they might enjoy a spree of sexual adventurousness that delivered heightened orgasms that seemed to go on forever.

In the night they spoke of their sexual fantasies and explored them all. They seemed driven to indulge in the sweet nectar of their come, which they drank like an elixir of the gods. Had it been possible they would have bathed in it, drowned in it, for this was lust that rode on the verge of death it was so powerful.

'Whoever said you can't have everything was wrong,' were James's last words before he fell fast asleep in Syrah's arms.

Chapter 11

Ira was an excellent chess player. It had always been an easy game for him because he had the ability to see a dozen moves ahead. He used logic and plotted his game in advance, studying his opponent's weaknesses and then using them to his own advantage. He was, besides, a man who could bide his time when he wanted something. His strength was that he rarely sacrificed a piece for the sake of moving forward. He played such a tight, ruthless game he rarely lost. For Ira, winning was the only option; to win big time an even better option. He conducted business in the same way and it had made him a very wealthy man, gained him the power to do pretty much whatever he wanted to do. His love life was handled in the same way. He was now an established name in property development, both in America and abroad.

Ira had known the Richebourg-Conti family socially for years. He had always envied the respect and the lifestyle Ethan enjoyed, the way he ran his wine empire and was accepted in every great house in Europe.

Right from first meeting Ethan, Ira had understood

that the man had no time for him. Disliked him even. To circumvent that dislike he'd cultivated a friendship with Caleb and Paula. He secretly considered them ninnies but envied Caleb because he and all the world knew that one day he would inherit the Richebourg-Conti vineyards and the prestige that accompanied their label, which was no small thing.

He saw Caleb and Paula champing at the bit to diversify, to strike out on their own and out from under what they saw as Ethan's autocratic rule. That was how the three of them had begun to do business together. It was not difficult to see that the couple's greed was such that the lust for a deal, rather than good business sense, governed their every move, their every investment. It had been several years since their relationship had turned into a business one. Ira was amazed that so far they did not seem to have realised that it was he who was gaining all the power, the best of any deal, rather than them. It was not that they were being foolish or making bad investments, merely that because they were always overextending themselves they allowed Ira to grab the largest slice of every deal. Now, with Ethan's death and the loss of the cellar and Ruy Blas, Caleb and Paula were approaching him to bail them out of their problems at Richebourg-Conti with an injection of capital. Now was the time for Ira to make his move. A ready-made checkmate deal if ever he saw one.

For more than two years he had been plotting and planning to take over Richebourg-Conti. He wanted the vineyard for himself and his French partner and now saw himself in a strong position to get what he wanted: the greedy Caleb and Paula could be forced out. Syrah too had no idea what she was doing and could not hold out financially long enough even to bring in her first harvest. She too was ripe for takeover.

Those were the things going through his mind as he sat in the Polo Lounge of the Beverly Hills Hotel, waiting for his latest love interest to arrive: eighteen years old and on the cover of *Vogue* this month. For a fleeting moment he thought of Diana. She would always be there in the background of his life. The waiter filled his glass with champagne. And Syrah . . . he had always fantasised about conquering her. She remained an itch that had to be scratched.

It was personal, sexual, a fascinating challenge to win her over to him in bed. And who knew? Maybe one day even to the altar. But he never mixed business *and* pleasure, and for the moment Syrah remained very much business. He smiled to think of the hardship she was putting herself through trying to keep Ruy Blas, the difficulties Caleb and Paula were constantly contriving to put her in. It was time once more to move in on Syrah. He would make her an offer she could not refuse.

Ira looked at his watch then towards the entrance to the Lounge. Tiffany Cole was an hour late. Suddenly she appeared and every eye was upon her as she wove through the tables to join him. She was so very sexy, so obviously fire and ice in the bedroom stakes yet somehow vacuous otherwise. He rose from his chair and kissed her on the cheek, caressed her amazingly beautiful long blonde hair, and whispered in her ear: 'You're too late for lunch.'

Tiffany was still confused when he shoved her into a taxi and told her, 'Next time don't play your feminine tricks on me.' He slammed the door shut and told the driver, 'Take the lady wherever she wants to go,' handing him a fifty-dollar note. Ira watched her sobbing and crying as the taxi pulled away from the curb. One of the many things he had loved about Diana was that she never played female power games with him.

Three hours after drinking champagne, in the Polo Lounge, Ira was on a private Gulf Stream Jet with his secretary, personal assistant and lawyer en route for France for a meeting with his French associate. Baron Michel de Brilliant Vivier, whose château had lent its name to his premier cru claret, had, together with Ira, been plotting the takeover of Richebourg-Conti and how to buy out every other small vineyard in the Napa Valley that came on the market.

For some time the Baron's intention had been to move in on the California wine industry and for Château Brilliant Vivier to become as great a force in the States as it was in France. Ira wanted to become the most powerful landowner in Northern California. The two men believed they had a partnership made in heaven. It had been a long hard struggle to get into the strong position they now held and Ira was flushed with excitement about the last move.

He had called the Baron and told him, 'Once Richebourg-Conti and Richebourg-Ruy Blas are ours, we'll have that invincible foothold in the industry and jumping off point for the American Château Brilliant Vivier you have been waiting for. I'm flying over for a meeting to put you in the picture and discuss our final moves.'

Their association had begun when the Baron had been introduced to Ira and told he was a Mr Fixit who could be a great ally in his quest to establish himself in a big way in California. The two men quickly realised their ambitions meshed one into the other. It was Ira who put the package together for a partnership between them. It entailed a thirty per cent stake in the profits for Ira, seventy for the Baron, and Ira owning the land which he would lease for ninety-nine years to their company.

Ira dreamed up the deal and approached the Baron with it when he heard the other man was ready to move on a similar arrangement in South Africa. Time, energy and money had been expended on putting the South African deal together, but California was more tempting. It had been costly for the Baron to change horses but he was a shrewd businessman as well as first-class wine man. He saw the advantages of expansion into California and most especially owning Ethan Richebourg's famous vineyards.

The Baron admired Ira Rudman for his successes and his ruthlessness. He liked the good-looking American who had polished manners and a certain charm and wit that was more continental than American. He saw Ira as a good partner but had never been quite sure he could deliver all he promised: the Richebourg vineyards and winery. The Baron had known Ethan for forty years and a finer wine connoisseur had not existed. Dead or alive he was still a powerful influence in California and acquiring his vineyards would not be easy. The Baron had made it clear to Ira that money and time were prime factors in their deal together. That was the pressure he'd placed on Ira and stayed firm about.

While the two men needed each other to get what each of them wanted, the Baron liked to hedge his business deals. At the last minute in his partnership negotiations with Ira he had sprung a penalty clause into their deal. Hence the rush to confer with him.

He and his Rolls Royce were waiting on the tarmac as Ira's plane taxied to a stop. All the way from the private airport to Paris and the Plaza Athenée where Ira always stayed it was just pleasant chit-chat and introductions to the staff he had brought with him.

The Baron had to admire Ira, who looked relaxed and full of enthusiasm. He had slept on the plane for most of the flight, shaved and showered, and there was not a wrinkle to be seen in his clothes nor any indication of jet lag.

Once they drove up to the entrance of the hotel, it was his suggestion that the staff should check in while he and the Baron went on to lunch at Le Grand Véfour, where he had taken the liberty of making a reservation. The

Baron was inwardly amused. Paris might be his territory but Ira never missed a trick. He was in control of whatever he had come to see the Baron about and that even extended to organising lunch.

If it was a matter of one upmanship, which the Baron could never understand, once in the famous restaurant at the Palais Royal Ira was losing hands down. The fuss made over the Baron's dining there was considerable but discreet. Over Ira? More elaborate, more obvious, the sort saved only for Americans.

Once seated and a sumptuous meal ordered by Ira, the wines chosen by the Baron, Ira put him in the picture about what was going on vis-à-vis their takeover. There was no doubt that he had done a brilliant job in gaining a controlling interest in Richebourg-Conti and the Baron could understand his excitement over at last taking over the company and booting out Caleb and Paula.

'And Ruy Blas? Ethan's cellar? When will the girl sign them over to us?' asked the Baron.

'As soon as I take over Richebourg-Conti,' answered Ira.

'You are certain of that?'

'Yes, it's merely a matter of when.'

'Well, that could be a problem for you, Ira. Is that what this meeting is about?'

'Hardly! Time is still on my side. I came to see you because I wanted you to know I am putting in hand our takeover of Richebourg-Conti in the next few days. That will shake the Californian wine world! I thought you should prepare to be revealed as the mystery buyer. You and I need to talk about how we'll proceed once that is accomplished. I don't mind telling you, I feel on top of the world about this takeover and so should you.'

'The deal is nothing to me without Ruy Blas, Ira. It has always been the very heart of Richebourg-Conti. I won't be satisfied until I have every one of the Richebourg vineyards. I'm sure I don't need to remind you that our agreement states you must deliver the deeds to the Richebourg vineyards and winery, Ethan's cellar included, on a specific date. The delays in moving into California have cost me dearly so you can appreciate how thrilled I am to hear the move is imminent. I admit it, Ira, I could never have done the deal without you,' said the Baron as he lit his cigar.

Both men knew that Château Brilliant Vivier would become an immediate threat to the several French labels already established in the Napa Valley. That was why the Baron had remained in the background of the deal. Those other French wine houses would have competed mercilessly to keep Château Brilliant Vivier out of California.

The men parted after lunch and agreed to meet the following morning before Ira took off once more for California. He refused a ride to his hotel. Instead he took a walk in the Tuileries then sat down on one of the park's benches and thought about his next moves.

In fact time was running out for Ira as well as Caleb and Paula. Syrah . . . The penalty clause that the Baron had so shrewdly insisted upon before he would sign the partnership agreement made between them stated that Ira must pay Château Brilliant Vivier one million dollars a day for every day the deeds were not delivered after a stipulated date. The penalty clause was to be invoked for eighty days at the end of which their partnership agreement would become null and void.

Ira had not felt he was taking such a gamble when he reluctantly accepted the last-minute clause the Baron had insisted upon. He was sure of his own cunning and the weakness and greed of Caleb and Paula, their lack of experience in high-stakes wheeling and dealing. But he could never have imagined that Ethan would split Ruy Blas from Richebourg-Conti and leave it to Syrah. Even when that did happen, knowing her character and the lifestyle she'd enjoyed, he had not been too concerned about the penalty clause. For him it was merely a side track that needed to be taken to get what he wanted. Ira believed Syrah had no work ethic, no ambition, she would sell her legacy and he would be the buyer.

Back in California Caleb and Paula waited anxiously for him to return their calls with the terms of a deal that would be advantageous to them. But Ira had vanished – gone abroad was what his office told them. For two whole days. Ira had never been unavailable to them, no matter where he had been, for such a length of time.

This absence was contrived, they were certain of that. It put the couple on edge, made them feel for the first time that they had to be more clever, drive a harder bargain with him than ever before. They were in the drawing room of Château Richebourg-Conti when for the first time Caleb realised he might possibly be on the verge of losing the family home. He rose from his chair and walked around. He had always coveted the things in the drawing room; they were beautiful and rare and yet never merely for display. Always just his home.

Standing at the fireplace, he said, 'We need Syrah's vineyard and the cellar more than ever to make a better deal with Ira.'

'Well, we know that! And we'll get them, one way or another. But it would be good to remember that whatever deal we make with Ira, he needs us just as much as we need him. He is, after all, no wine man. What good would Richebourg-Conti be to him without us running it?' said his wife, a note of irritation in her voice.

'That's what worries me. I know you're not as passionate about the vineyards and winery as I am. Every move we have made to diversify has been right but we're essentially wine people,' Caleb rambled on.

'What are you talking about, Caleb?' she asked, more annoyed with him than ever.

'I'm frightened – frightened of what's happening to Richebourg-Conti. Or at least I will be until the deal is made with Ira. For me Richebourg-Conti has always meant more than wine and success and vineyards. It's my heritage, the continuity of all the Richebourgs who immigrated from France to cross the West and establish themselves in California. I've suddenly remembered that.'

Paula rose from her chair and went to stand next to her husband. 'I love the vineyards and the winery just as much as you do, Caleb. You can't, after so many years of having me working by your side for Richebourg-Conti, believe otherwise. But we have always wanted more from this place, to move with the times, for it to become even more profitable, create things with its revenues. We have done well for ourselves using the power of the Richebourg-Conti name, which we have enjoyed to the fullest, but that power could have been doubled or trebled had Ethan given us our chance to expand and that's what is going to happen for us now. You'll see. I trust Ira. He's too greedy for us not to do well out of this.

'I enjoy to the full my lifestyle: working with you as a co-director of Richebourg-Conti, sitting on the boards of two museums, raising funds for the Republican Party, sponsoring two university seats, doing the lecture circuit talking about wine for the Napa Valley Wine Association, living in a grand house in a grand manner.

'Don't you think I know I only hold those positions because of who I am, what I have? Do you think for a minute I'll allow Ira or that bitch of a sister of yours to take one bit of that away from me, no matter what they're wanting or plotting. Not on your life or mine, my darling husband. Get what's mine? I think not! Nor is what we have enough. I want more. And most of all I want Ruy Blas. We need it, yes, but that's not the only reason why we should never let Syrah have it. She doesn't *deserve* it, hasn't earned it as we have, because she got a fortune from Ethan that was rightfully ours as well as hers.'

Caleb listened. How many hundreds of times had he heard his wife's rhetoric? But this was the first time he realised she was more intent on depriving Syrah of her legacy than he was. He was so stunned that he said nothing, merely walked from the room, lost in thoughts about himself and his wife. On the porch he sat on the top step and viewed the glorious vista of Richebourg-Conti. His Richebourg-Conti. He loved it more desperately than ever he had.

He felt like a drowning man as his life flashed before him. He had always seen himself and his wife as having very different personalities; his had been a softer, more generous heart. He'd had a more passive nature when they had met and had fallen instantly in love. He'd admired her strength and her passion, above all her ambition. Living with her had made him hard and ruthless and he had loved the fact that she had instilled that in him. He had loved her blindly and allowed her to dominate him, his life, his work.

He loved her even more because of her devotion to their children, her ambition and expertise in working alongside him in Richebourg-Conti as well as being a loving wife and mother. Such behaviour had convinced him he could never live without her, and that was how her every wish became his command. Over the years her every ambition became his. But what he had not realised until now was that it had come about because of his fear of losing her and a desire above all for peace to reign in his marriage.

Paula had seen something in Caleb's eyes as he had walked from the room. Had it been pain, anxiety, or the weakness in him she so despised and yet loved him for because he always conquered it to please her? His weaknesses excited something in Paula. She actually loved him on many counts: he gave her a life she might never have had without him and which she liked very much indeed, he was a marvellous father to their children and, while not an imaginative lover, their sex life was all she could ever want and more. And she loved him because he allowed her complete control of their lives and always had.

It was this obsessive need to control that made Paula reach a decision. She would approach Syrah with a deal, one she would surely not refuse. It still niggled that Caleb had gone to Malibu without her to make that first offer to buy his sister out. Nothing would have brought Richebourg-Conti to the state it was in now had the spoiled brat sold out to them then.

The following morning, much to the relief of Caleb and Paula, Ira called, suggesting a meeting to discuss Richebourg-Conti. Paula took the call and was not terribly pleased with the tone of his voice or the manner in which he spoke to her. It was friendly, polite enough, but sharp and to the point. It was his manner that made her refuse to see him straight away and put him off for five days. He accepted her date and time but was curt about it.

Paula took it upon herself, as a last resort, to meet

Syrah. The invitation was to a talk over lunch. Paula had chosen a small, out-of-the-way inn, believing that this meeting would be best held on neither side's territory.

She was already there, seated at a table, when Syrah arrived. As she walked towards her sister-in-law she had to admit that Paula was a beauty and could understand her brother's passion for her. But it was a cold, rigid sort of beauty, sexual but mean of heart. Once Syrah was at the table, Paula looked up from the menu she was reading.

'Thank you for coming, Syrah. We should have done this directly after Ethan's death,' were her first words.

Syrah took the other seat at the table. Paula snapped her fingers at the waiter. He rushed to her signal and she ordered drinks for them both.

'You remember what I drink?' said Syrah.

'Why so surprised? I remember many things about you. Shall we order?'

'I suppose we'd better. That *is* what we're here for, to have lunch and try to mend broken fences, isn't it?' answered Syrah.

'That's quite an assumption and it's wrong. To make you a very wealthy woman – that's why we're here,' said Paula expansively.

Syrah began to laugh. 'Now how do you expect to do that? Make me an offer for the legacy Ethan left me? Don't even try. It's not and never will be for sale.'

'Fifty million dollars, cash, delivered to you within three days,' Paula pressed on.

'No! You don't listen, Paula. You and Caleb can never

have Ruy Blas or Ethan's wine cellar. If he had wanted you to have them, he would have left them to you. I have wondered for a long time why he left them to me. Now I've worked it out and you had better too. That said, I did come here believing you might want to end this feud going on between us and become a family again. Maybe not as loving as I might like but at least friends. Caleb is my brother after all,' added Syrah.

Paula could barely contain herself. For several seconds she remained silent while years of resentment, pure hatred for Syrah, rose like bile within her. The thousand and one instances when Syrah and Ethan had, throughout her life, been cruel to her swept like a rushing stream before her eyes.

Finally she spoke. When she did she was out of control. 'Friendship? With you? You're as stupid and insensitive as you have always been, I see. You are behaving true to form: the selfish, self-centred, playgirl whore funded by a daddy who loved you too much – incestuously for all I know – and even after death left you what was rightfully Caleb's and mine. We need that legacy Ethan threw away on you, but do you care? Not even for fifty million dollars.'

Paula never let up. She seemed to gather strength in her vindictiveness by grinding Syrah into the ground. Beaten into submission she could not even find the strength to rise from her chair and leave. It was Paula who finally walked away from the table, shaking with rage, leaving Syrah on her own to deal with this abuse.

Chapter 12

James Whitehawk was dining at a small table in a corner of the restaurant when first Paula and then Syrah were shown to their table. Neither of the women had seen him. The scene between them was embarrassing for the few other diners in the room. Once Paula had taken her leave, James went over to Syrah and drew a chair up to sit next to her.

As it had been for them in the garden at Richebourg-Conti and every time since, when they were together, the outside world fell away and the joy of life, the strong erotic attraction they felt for each other, was paramount. What they were together wiped out all thoughts of the hideous meeting Syrah had just endured. James took a room for them in the picturesque town that was reminiscent of St Paul de Vence in the South of France.

There seemed no point in discussing what had happened between Syrah and Paula. The incredible coincidence of James having been there too was more important, more meaningful, something full of love, instead of the hatred of a soulless, greedy woman. They spoke of their incredible luck in finding one another, how the intimacy they felt together was stronger than either one of them. Then they stopped talking and made love, had sex that was thrilling and filled with passion, the desire to pleasure each other, again and again.

Ready to leave, they could not bear to be apart and so Syrah left her car in the village, to be retrieved by one of James's workers, and he drove them back to Ruy Blas.

Leaning against him, Syrah told him in a soft and sensual voice, 'I am always very much aware that there is something about our togetherness that is thrilling and mysterious, the adventure of a lifetime that neither of us will ever truly understand.'

It had been some time now since James and Syrah had become an open secret, a permanent presence in each other's life around the vineyards, their wine friends and Keoki. New joys were added to their relationship when James decided that his daughters Betsy and Carrie, should become part of their lives and brought them round to play with Keoki. He wanted Syrah and her son to have a chance to learn to love his girls as he did.

Always cautious, never wanting to offend, as the children moved in on their lives, James and Syrah kept their sexual life played out in romantic meetings in hideaways and were discreet because Katherine Whitehawk was more dangerous to them now than ever. She had found out James was having an intimate relationship with Syrah.

In those weeks when Syrah was seeing other men,

James's life became unbearable, full of fear that she might indeed find someone and finally leave him, against her will but because she wanted to have a full, rich life shared with a man who was hers and hers alone. James's fear drove him once more to ask Katherine to set him free.

It had come about one evening when they were dining at home. Betsy and Carrie, having finished their dinner, went to their rooms to do homework. Katherine and James were sitting at the head and the foot of the long mahogany dining table. Candles were burning in their tall silver sticks, the antique Chinese wall paper glowed softly and the marble commodes and Ming Dynasty jardinières were dazzlingly impressive. This was James's favourite room in the house, though there was not one he did not like.

Beautiful houses had always been a part of Katherine's life, she had been born into them whereas James had not. When they had fallen in love it had been their differences that had seduced each of them. She was fine as porcelain, complex, feminine and needy for something James thought he could give her. She demanded one hundred per cent attention from him, had thought he would pander to her every whim, that there would be no other life or friends, just the two of them together for always. He had never understood that and she'd spent her entire life from the day they had met trying to change him into the image of him she had created in her own mind.

As James gazed down the table, past the peonies and the flickering candle flames, not for the first time he wondered why the beautiful and elegant Katherine would not let him go. There were an infinite number of men who had courted her once and would still. Men who could make her happy. He could only believe what their years together had shown him, that her fragile, deeply disturbed mind, with its twists and turns, demanded that they should remain married, no matter the hatred and unhappiness between them.

'I want to talk to you, Katherine,' he told her as he rose from his chair and went to sit next to her.

She looked at her husband. She still found him handsome, still sexy. For a fleeting moment she thought she might seduce him into her bed right then and there. He never could resist her sexually. He yearned for her, and that was why she teased and taunted him with her flirting, why she never let him have her unless it was to torture him about his inadequacies as a husband, the man who should care for her no matter what.

'To say you're sorry, beg my forgiveness for being such a cheating bastard?' she asked.

'No. To ask you for a divorce. There's no point in our staying together,' he answered.

'I would say two daughters might be the point.'

'Don't do that, Katherine. I beg you, don't deprive me of my children's love. This is nothing to do with them. This is something between us. You keep using them as a shield to hide behind, blackmailing me with them.'

'Yes, I do. And so what?' she replied.

'If you could only hear yourself! Don't you love them? How can you do this to them, use them to keep me in line?'

'Oh, that's easily explained. I'm obsessive and unbalanced about you, James. Always have been since that first night we met. I want you to love me the way *I* want to be loved. For you to give up your life for me, stand by me in everything I do, give me everything I want. You never have unless blackmailed to do so. Why do you want a divorce anyway? To marry Syrah Richebourg?'

With that Katherine scraped back her chair and, rising from it, threw her dinner napkin in her husband's face. She didn't wait for an answer. Instead she stalked angrily away. Halfway between the table and the door she stopped and turned round to face her husband. James rose from his chair. He recognised a certain wildness, an out-of-control look in her eyes. Katherine at her most dangerous.

'No divorce for you, my handsome Indian brave. Not even a separation. I have no problem with the world knowing Syrah Richebourg is a whore who can't keep her hands off my husband. How you must hate her having to live a backstreet life with you! That does give me some little satisfaction, I admit.'

Then she turned on her heel and walked from the room. James sat down in his chair and poured himself a glass of wine. He sipped it and contemplated his situation. His wife was on a knife edge. All through dinner he had seen signs of her slowly slipping off the rails of sanity. Hatred was now pathological with her. She was frightening in her madness – and there was no doubt in James's mind that she *was* a mad woman, though for most of the time had control of her madness. Paradoxically, the more bizarre her behaviour, the more beautiful and sweet she appeared. Tonight at dinner she had looked so lovely, been so nasty.

Throughout the evening she hardly let up for a minute on Betsy and Carrie with constant criticism and threats of retribution if they did not obey her every command: they should eat more slowly, faster, no playing with their food. At one point Carrie, the younger of the girls, had answered back and Katherine leaned forward and pinched her wrist so hard that the child screamed, broke away and ran to James. He had seen it all before, this love-hate thing she had had right from the time the children had been born. They were why he took the abuse he did from her. The safety of his children, their love and their happiness, was everything to James.

Finally he went to Katherine's bedroom where he found her lying on a chaise-longue reading. She did not look up from her book. He walked directly to her and snatched it from her hands, throwing it across the room. Then, grabbing her by the wrist, he pulled her from the chaise to stand next to him and held her in a tight grip. She struggled to free herself but in vain. Tears of frustration came to her eyes and she was breathing hard.

'If I ever catch you abusing the girls again as you did this evening, I will kidnap them from you and go directly to the police. I will declare you an unfit mother and give the media the sorry story of how a society beauty such as yourself, a worker for so many children's charities, is a loveless and sadistic mother, mentally unbalanced by adoration of herself and no other human being.

'Oh, I'll stay with you. Syrah is happy to be my mistress so that vindictiveness of yours means nothing to her. You see, it is and always has been for the girls that I remain. You threaten to turn them against me, true, that's one reason why I stay with you. Another is that I fear for their safety, even were I to leave and take them with me. But the final reason is because they love their mother, make excuses for your meanness to them, are always defending your cruelty in one pathetic way after another. They are loving and caring girls and they know how unhappy you are and only want to make you well and have you love them.'

James released his wife and pushed her away. She sat down hard on the chaise and hissed back at him: 'You are a puppet of a man, James, and I still pull the strings. You would do well to remember that.'

He went from her bedroom to the girls' rooms. With the help of their nanny he packed their school uniforms and some toys. 'We're going to stay the night at Keoki's house,' he told them. 'Nanny is coming too. Let's be quiet about it, though.' Glee appeared on the girls' faces. This was a game for them and so they tiptoed round the room and, still in their night dresses and wrapped in their robes, stole from the house.

The months following that night were busy for Syrah. James, her work, all the pressures and financial problems, the coming and going of James's children, the excitement of studying wine so that she might become one of the two hundred odd Masters of Wine, her fight with her colleagues against the land developers in the valley, her flying work, all gave her a life that was rewarding but undeniably hectic. She often wondered what she had done with her life before Ethan's death had changed it for her. She'd seemed to seek nothing yet remarkably everything had come to her. Though always pinched for money, at times not knowing where she would find next week's housekeeping, Syrah was having the happiest, most fascinating time of her life. Until a cloud in the form of James's wife cast a dark shadow.

It came without warning months after James had arrived unexpectedly with the girls and their nanny to stay the night. He had told Syrah about the scene at dinner that had convinced him his wife was now so emotionally twisted and out of control that he saw her as not only a danger to his children but to Syrah and even to herself. He had begged Syrah that night to be cautious if ever Katherine should suddenly appear. But she never had appeared nor had she done anything to be annoying to Syrah. Like everyone else, as time passed and nothing happened, Syrah tended to think James might be exaggerating his wife's neurotic behaviour. And then one day, as Syrah was pushing a wheelbarrow loaded with rubbish from the vineyard past the entrance to Ethan's wine cellar, there leaning against a yellow Porsche stood Katherine.

Syrah stopped a few feet away from the woman and wiped her brow with a red spotted handkerchief she retrieved from round her neck. Though she had never seen Katherine Whitehawk, instinct told her immediately who this beautiful petite woman was. Seeing her there, seeing her at all, did come as a surprise. Syrah had not imagined that Katherine was as charismatic as she appeared to be. There was, apart from her beauty, a seductive quality about her that made Syrah understand why James must have been enchanted by her. Why her daughters praised their mother even when they were victims of her wickedness. She emanated a certain honey-coated nastiness that disconcerted Syrah. It might have been merely the fact that she was confronting Syrah on her home ground and without warning. Or could it be that that beauty of hers was obviously combined with a wide streak of self-absorption. Yes, thought Syrah, she is dangerous because she uses people up and leaves them broken by her selfishness.

The two women stood eye to eye, taking the measure of each other, before Katherine broke the silence. She was icily civilised but menacing when she addressed Syrah. 'The wife confronting the mistress . . . cheap novelette stuff, not worthy of my time or my emotions, so I will come straight to the point. My husband says he loves you. My girls adore you and your son. On the other hand your feuds with your brother and his wife are common gossip and most embarrassing. You have made no social inroads to assure you of some standing in this community. So I strongly suggest you sell out and leave the valley.

'You see, I will never divorce James, you will never be any more than a mistress to him. You will however gain a reputation for alienating me from him and my children, which is in fact exactly what you're doing. Remain here and usurp my position with my husband and family and I guarantee I will see to it you are labelled a whore and your dirty laundry hung out for all to see. You may not care about that but your bastard son will.'

'Your threats are wasted on me. I will never give James up. It's enough for me to know he would like to marry me. I love him and your girls and will gladly be part of an extended family for them. Give them the love you ration out to them depending on your mood swings. My love is unconditional. Now we've met and we both know where we stand. There's nothing more to say so I suggest you leave my vineyard and never attempt to return.' Having said her piece Syrah walked to the door on the driver's side of the Porsche and opened it.

Katherine walked up to her and said, 'I think you should know that I hold the purse strings of a vast fortune, if that is what you're after, so forget any money coming from James. It would also be better if you behaved more properly towards me because I know how to make James suffer and, rest assured, I *will* make him suffer for his disloyalty to me. I am clever when I am deliberately nasty and I am only nasty deliberately. I warn you, I will be that way, like plucking feathers off a humming bird, until none of you can bear it any longer. In time the end will come for you and James and you will give each other up.'

She slipped past Syrah into the driver's seat of her car and calmly reached out to close the door. Her last words were, 'He's mine. 'Til death do us part.' Then she started the engine and slowly drove away.

Katherine was as good as her word. After months of subtle nastiness to him, Syrah, the girls and even Keoki, she managed to eat away at their happiness. Fear crept in and crippled their love. No matter how much James and Syrah loved each other they could find no justification for staying together at the children's expense. Fearing for Betsy and Carrie and what Katherine's campaign of hatred was doing to them they began to drift apart, to face the reality of what was happening to and around them.

They and the children were having a few days fishing in the mountains above the Valley. They had spent a glorious day riding to the lake where James had built a cabin. It was rough with no gas, electricity, or even running water. They fished for their dinner and sat round a fire afterwards. All day long Syrah kept standing back and viewing the fishing party. This was the family she had always wanted for Keoki. There were bonds between Carrie, Betsy and her son, between Syrah and the girls. And James? His was the strength that kept them together. Syrah felt a wrench to her heart. This was how it should always be and was not. Most of the time they were, in one way or another, each and every one of them fighting off a hostile force that was trying to destroy what they had together. She knew in her heart then that it had to be over for them, for the sake of their children and the lengths Katherine might go to to harm them.

With the children all tucked into bed in the cabin and fast asleep, James turned down the oil lamps. Syrah and he stood silently watching them for several minutes then returned to sit outside opposite each other across a fire shooting sparks and a trail of smoke upward to a black sky studded with a myriad of stars. It had been such a perfect family day out, far from the stress they were usually under down in the Valley.

'This day, this night, is surely what we want for our children?' Sarah began. 'Not in isolated incidents to cling on to but as life itself. They're too young to be caught up in our love for each other, the pain and anxiety that Katherine inflicts upon us through them. I am battle weary from trying to protect them. James, we must break off this affair and I think we both know that. Your wife will never stop mentally and physically abusing the children as long as we are together. A clean break is called for. Half measures won't do. We tried that.'

He remained silent for some time, too choked with emotion to speak. He knew Syrah was right. In the months since Katherine had paid her visit to Ruy Blas and confronted Syrah he had gone down many paths: lawyers, psychiatrists, child therapists, the head mistress of their school, seeking help for his wife and his children. He had even put the police on notice of Katherine's erratic behaviour so that if the children should ever call them for help they were in the picture and would come to their aid. All in secret so as not to antagonise Katherine for fear she might become even more vindictive, do more than hurt the children. She had actually warned James that she could and might take her own life, and the girls' along with her.

'I will never love anyone else, Syrah,' he managed now.

'Nor I, James, and that is what must keep us apart and give us the courage to find happiness wherever we can: in a sunset, a good meal, laughter, day-to-day living. Otherwise our sacrifice will have been for nothing.'

Two days later, as they broke camp to return to the Valley, over a picnic by the lake James spoke to the three children. 'Syrah and I have been talking. We both agreed this was the best family outing we have ever had.'

The children broke in, citing several incidents as proof. Their faces were filled with glee and there was laughter, and tickles for Keoki.

James carried on, 'You know Syrah and I would like it to be this way always?'

Once more he was interrupted. 'Me too, me too,' cried each of the children.

Syrah thought her heart would break, seeing their enthusiasm, their innocence in believing that such a possibility existed. She had to look away to bring herself under control. She knew that James and she had to discuss the break-up with the children so they did not feel rejected but it was more painful for her than she had thought it would be.

James continued, 'Now I know you three are really grown up so we can talk to you about several things.'

The smiles disappeared from their young faces and they were attentive at once. Syrah could actually see the light-hearted glint in their eyes dim. 'Have we done something wrong?' asked Keoki.

'No, not a single thing. The problem is we're living like a happy normal family and it's not true. We are a make-believe family. Because we all love each other and want to be together we're having to fight off nasty gossip about us. Mostly you children. You girls are having to take mental and at times physical abuse from your mother. I know what price you are all three paying so Syrah and I can be together and you can be part of our lives.

'Syrah and I don't want to live a make-believe life. There's more to be considered, not least your mother, girls. I know you love her and she's as much a part of your life as I am. We all know she is in some ways no longer accountable for her behaviour. We have to help her to be happy and whole again. Syrah agrees with that, so she and I have decided to go our separate ways and try for another life without each other.

'That does not mean we love each other or you children any the less. It only means that this is the last time we will all be together. A clean break will make it easier for us all. Now we have to kiss each other goodbye, and

212

remember we are and always will be the best of friends in our minds and hearts.'

And for the first time since Syrah had inherited Ruy Blas, James was no longer there by her side.

Chapter 13

The meeting between Ira, Paula and Caleb could hardly have been considered a success from anyone's point of view. No deal could be struck because no one had managed to convince Syrah to sell her legacy. Ira made it clear to Caleb and Paula that the bail out was going to cost them dearly. He put the pressure on them to get Ruy Blas and the wine cellar at any price. Time was running out for Richebourg-Conti and the private fortune Caleb and Paula had sunk into deals with Ira. But time was running out for him as well. The penalty clause in his agreement with the Baron was looming as was the due date for the closing of their deal and the take-over of Richebourg-Conti. But characteristically he calmly and determinedly tackled his problems.

The most interesting thing to come out of the meeting between them was the news that James and Syrah had broken up and this time for good. That came straight from Katherine Whitehawk and was confirmed when Caleb learned that James was no longer seen round Ruy Blas or advising Syrah. Now more than ever he was certain he could win her over.

Ira was still sexually smitten with her, obsessively so. His obsession immediately went into overdrive on hearing that James was obviously out of her life. More so than ever Ira saw Syrah as easy prey: her poverty, the struggle to work her vineyard and better her wine production, competing against Caleb and Paula, made her vulnerable and most especially so without James to lean on. He saw this as the moment to move in on her for romance but, more importantly, to offer to buy her legacy. Enough time had passed for her to feel the difficulty of the hard road she had so rashly decided to take. Ira was certain she was ripe now to curtail the hardships she was putting herself through.

It was easy for him to call Syrah because he had never believed in her new passion for Ruy Blas and the wine world she professed to find so exciting. He had always let her rejection of him roll over him as if it had never happened. He was one of those men who never understood the word no.

Luck seemed to be on his side. It was Syrah who answered her telephone. A shiver of delight ran through his body as he heard her voice.

'Hello, Syrah, it's Ira.'

She hesitated before she answered, 'What do you want, Ira?'

'What I've always wanted. The legacy Ethan left and you for myself,' he told her.

She had to laugh at his audacity. 'Well, at least you're

honest. You can forget it on both counts, Ira. Oh, and please don't call me again, no matter what the deal may be.' She hung up on him.

Ira called back immediately. Before he could say a word she asked, 'Are you going to be a nuisance about this, Ira?'

'No, just hear me out. I want to take you to dinner – business, social, call it what you may. There are things you should know about Richebourg-Conti, things that if Ethan were alive he would want you to be aware of. I'm not doing this out of the generosity of my heart but because it might change your determination to struggle on at Ruy Blas.'

Not dinner but a business lunch had been Syrah's decision. Not wanting him anywhere near Ruy Blas, she agreed to dine with him at Spago in Los Angeles. He sent a small jet for her and his Bentley was waiting to whisk her to the restaurant. Such luxuries had been her usual lifestyle before Ethan's death. She slipped back into a role she knew well: not having to deal with the mundane. She smiled as the city flashed by her windows and said aloud, 'Ira, devil incarnate, this is great but no longer interesting to me, you bastard.'

The restaurant buzzed with Hollywood celebrities, Californian millionaires doing deals, beautiful well-dressed women of all ages looking as delicious as it was possible to be. Ira watched Syrah as she approached his table. She looked radiantly beautiful in her black linen dress and high-heeled shoes, a long red chiffon scarf tied round her neck and trailing voluptuously behind her.

When he rose from his chair to greet her, he said, 'It's marvellous to see you.'

'I wish I could say the same, Ira, but I can't. I'm only here because of what you said I must know about what's going on at Richebourg-Conti.'

'Before we get into that I want you to know that my desire to own and be a part of Richebourg-Conti and Ruy Blas is one thing but my passion for you is another. Don't lie to yourself or me. I know the erotic attraction between us is mutual.'

'You're dreaming, Ira. What about Diana? She's finished with you and yet for me to go to bed with you would not only be distasteful to me but, I feel, disloyal to her. So just put that out of your mind and let's get on with whatever you have to tell me.'

Ira listened and Syrah's every word did nothing but feed his obsession to possess her totally. 'What about Diana? You ask. She still loves me and one day will return to me. You are something apart from my relationship with her, but all that could change. I am fast falling in love with you. I know there is a deep and long-lasting friendship between you two, and that can remain. It need not have any effect on the intimate life between you and me. I want you for yourself, Syrah, and your legacy for us.'

'My God! You're a devious bastard, Ira. Forget it, I'm not interested in a sex life with you or any other man I'm not in love with.'

'Now don't tell me you're going to turn celibate just because you can't have James Whitehawk? Come off it, I know what a strong libido you have.'

'Now you're sounding cross, and I thought you were above that. My mistake. Do you or don't you have business to discuss with me?'

'You should make it up with Caleb and Paula and sell them your legacy if you will not sell it to me. They have been too greedy and ambitious and are in great trouble. They're looking for me to bail them out with an enormous injection of capital. When I do, they'll have lost Richebourg-Conti. Now if you don't want to see that happen you have no choice but to sell Ruy Blas and Ethan's wine cellar to them or to me.

'There's nothing vindictive in this, it's just another hostile business takeover. I needed you to know the position because in spite of what you think, I do care for you and Keoki, I do want you to enjoy the life you once had and for your struggles to be over.'

The very thought of the family losing Richebourg-Conti was so frightful, Syrah could have broken down and wept in the restaurant. Ira could see how the news had affected her, she had grown pale and seemed dazed. She was also aware that she was in the most frightful position and could no longer call on James for advice on what to do. She had the good sense to realise this was not the time or the place or the person to talk business with. One day she would no doubt have to, and through lawyers. Her anger was not against Ira but Caleb and Paula. That they should ever have dealt with Ira had been bad enough but to have played into his hands so that now he could snatch Richebourg-Conti out from under them was unforgivable.

For the remainder of lunch Ira and Syrah agreed not to discuss the situation any further. She claimed she had to think things out and Ira, having delivered his blow, was more interested in Syrah as the object of his sexual fantasies.

She was clever enough to realise that though she was pulling back from Ira, it would do her no good to continue insulting and abusing him for being the monster he was. That was why when he told her he was going to fly back to the Valley with her, to work in the area where he hoped to buy several vineyards, she made no objection.

There was little she could do about his returning her to Ruy Blas but found it distasteful he should be on her land. As he helped her from the car, she said, 'You will understand if I don't show you around?' and was sorry she had even said that much because she saw the flash of anger come into his eyes.

Looking away from her to the vineyard Ira saw Diana working with some of the others on the vines. Once more he was aware of her as the only woman he had ever loved and felt a genuine admiration for: her honesty, her tremendous talent, natural sensuality, loyalty and a sweetness of heart.

Syrah and Ira watched her, both aware that for many years Diana had been the backbone of Ira's emotional life, the other side of his darkness, the corner of goodness that was not all business, ambition, ruthless greed. Syrah looked up at Ira and wondered if he still wanted to marry Diana, make babies with her, use her for what and who she was. He had always been blind to their differences that could never be resolved: his extravagance, her frugality; his ruthless business and political thinking, her liberal democratic beliefs; his pride and adoration of her as a cinema and theatre actress, her humility.

Watching Diana, Ira was contemplating how much he missed not being able to take possession of her sexually or when he needed a taste of genuine goodness and love. He disliked being estranged from Diana but still found it impossible to come to terms with her demands.

Ira's momentary distraction vanished like an apparition. Turning once more to Syrah, he concentrated his mind on her and the things he wanted most and was certain to get. He believed without a doubt that Syrah could not survive: her weaknesses, her repressed sexual attraction for him and her desperate need for money and relief from struggle would drive her into his arms, no matter what she might pretend.

'I have to leave now, Syrah, but one day I will take total possession of you, as I once did Diana, and I will own Ruy Blas. And soon. Sooner than you can imagine. You think about that,' he told her as he opened the car door.

'Soon, very soon,' he murmured as the car sped away from Ruy Blas. Time was running out and he had no intention of allowing himself to be ruined financially by a clever Frenchman and a penalty clause.

That night over dinner there seemed to be some tension between Diana and Syrah. They both knew that the cause was Ira's interest in Syrah but the two friends chose not to speak of it, Syrah because she believed that Diana was through with Ira once and for all. She had said so and continued to profess that her feelings for him were dead.

Tonight Diana remained silent about Ira because she had seen, and not for the first time, the sexual attraction between her friend and her former lover and knew that her long-standing friendship with Syrah had come between any affair they might have had. It was a situation she found too embarrassing to confront.

The two women were having a simple supper of sorrel soup and fresh bread from the local bakery, with a bottle of Riesling. Diana did of course know that Ira was once again after Ruy Blas. She could see how troubled Syrah was and asked, 'Do you want to tell me about it?'

'I think I'm in a hole so deep I'll never get out. Caleb and Paula have all but lost Richebourg-Conti. Ira insinuates that only I can save them with my legacy but that's merely a game of his, not fact,' Syrah told her.

Diana was not surprised. She had been working with Syrah and James for months, using her considerable fortune to help save the small growers in the vicinity who were struggling against phylloxera. Only that morning she had found out that Ira was about to steal the vineyard from Caleb and Paula unless Caleb was able to find the massive amount of money needed to buy him out.

Diana told Syrah what she knew and the two women sat well into the night over the bottle of wine, thinking of various ways they might save Richebourg-Conti. What they did agree was that neither Ira nor Caleb or Paula could make any immediate move without Syrah's co-operation and so they decided that for the moment the best thing was for her to get on with her work, the goals she had set herself, and be vigilant at all times.

It was the first anniversary of Ethan's death. Diana, Keoki and Syrah spent the day together, first in church and then in the cemetery to place flowers on his grave. At one point Keoki and Diana walked away so as to give Syrah some time on her own, close to her father. She no longer mourned his passing but missed him as desperately as ever. As she stood by his gravestone she sensed his warmth, his love, his pride in her and what she had done with her life. He gave her courage and strength and a sense that she had made all the right choices, possibly not the easiest but certainly the most rewarding. As she walked back towards Diana and Keoki she placed her hand on her heart. It ached for love, Ethan's, James's, but she was not sad. She had been loved by a father and a lover who had given her more than any woman can expect to have in a lifetime. If fate decreed that she had had enough, then so be it. She wanted no man other than James. Her sexual life was something she no longer even thought about. Desire had given way to memory and she had come to believe that that was better than sex with the wrong man. She was sure James felt the very same way. They were star-crossed lovers and she was learning to live with that.

Syrah's father had left her several wine diaries containing a wealth of trade secrets that had become invaluable to her. Information on growers, dealers and brokers, lists of people in the wine industry worldwide she could depend on and trust implicitly. The diaries had become a firm foundation for her studies on wine and the industry which by now was her primary interest in life after her son.

She and Keoki were still living in the shack, working their vineyard and selling off rare bottles of wine from the cellar when things were at their most desperate. Syrah was as busy as she could afford to be doing aerobatic flying and they were scraping by. All that was missing were those marvellous liaisons with James in remote places, where they could leave the world, and work, and all their problems behind them. Every day she longed for him and that edge of mystery and danger attached to their meetings which had so enhanced their time together.

Today was one of the times when she felt it almost unbearable that neither of them should know what was going on in the other's life. Indeed all that Syrah did know about James was that he was away from her and suffering as much as she was. What sustained her at moments such as these was her belief that one day when they were ready they would enter each other's lives again and live with each other and their children or grandchildren as the case may be.

Syrah's first harvest was a bumper crop and the finest of grapes. The first vintage offered since Ethan's death and under Syrah's own label was amazing, having been kept in its oak barrels, as suggested in Ethan's diary, for an extra two years. It was as good as the best of the superior wines ever produced with a Richebourg-Ruy Blas label.

Syrah was fast becoming a new but considerable name in the California wine industry: her working of Ruy Blas, the responsible and shrewd marketing of Ethan's wine collection, her diligent studying of wine in order to pass the Master of Wine examinations, and not least her work with the other small growers in the Napa Valley to keep Ira and other predators like him from swallowing them up, all commanded considerable respect.

People in the Napa and Sonoma Valley now talked about Syrah Richebourg's love and passion for wine and how intelligent she was about it. Many of the men in the trade, whether scholars, vintners or collectors, were astounded at her dedication and innate knowledge. Her name was now linked with Ethan's as a matter of course. They saw she had stepped into his shoes and believed in time she would be as respected a name as ever he was. To everyone, including Syrah, it was clear that Ethan had passed his mantle on to his daughter and had made no mistake in doing so.

Not a day slipped by that Syrah took for granted what

she had done in that year. Where had the courage come from, the strength of will to fight on against all odds? She had come to feel a profound love and pride in owning and working Ruy Blas, being a Richebourg. All that she had done, who and what she was, was giving her a greater understanding of how important it was that, though she and her family were split, at the very least Richebourg-Conti and Ruy Blas were owned by Richebourgs and that was the way it must always be.

Finally she had grown to believe what everyone said behind her back. Ethan had left her the legacy because he believed in his heart that she loved the vineyards as he did. He had known that she would never abuse his legacy to her the way Caleb would. He had taken a wild gamble on his daughter and had won. How had he known that she would be fulfilled in her life working on Ruy Blas?

For all the strides that Syrah was making, she had to be ever vigilant as to what was happening at Richebourg-Conti. No easy matter since she had to rely on gossip. To call Ira would be to put herself in the firing line and it was impossible to talk to anyone at Richebourg-Conti. It was Diana who heard the rumour that it was a matter of days before the banks foreclosed on Richebourg-Conti.

For the first time since Ethan's death Syrah returned to Château Richebourg-Conti for a meeting with Caleb, Paula and Ira. The three of them were openly hostile, Caleb and Paula still blaming her for their trouble. But this was a new and different Syrah. She listened to the usual abuse and then, ignoring them, addressed Ira.

226

'Take the pressure off Caleb and Paula, it will do you no good. I beg you not to go forward with this takeover of Richebourg-Conti. What good will it do you without Caleb? He at least knows the wine business, which you don't.'

Ira hung tough and told her, 'I don't need Caleb or Paula for that. What I need is your Ruy Blas and then everyone will benefit.'

'But mostly you! Ira, don't do this to the Richebourgs,' Syrah pleaded.

Things were getting more complex than Ira liked. He listened and all the time his mind kept working out a plan. He understood by the stance that Syrah was taking that if he were to close in and take over Richebourg-Conti she would most certainly not sell him Ruy Blas. That was the essential part of his deal with the Baron, and Ira had no intention of losing that deal and having to pay out eighty million dollars more than he had already invested in a takeover of Richebourg-Conti.

While Syrah was still talking he switched his plan, believing the way to go was to get Ruy Blas first and let it appear that he had backed off from his takeover of Richebourg-Conti. It was a moment of inspiration. He seized his chance. When Syrah stopped begging him for more time for Caleb and Paula to work out their problems it was easy for him to make his move because no matter what he said, however clever Caleb and Paula might try to be, he still had the trump card. He was at that moment the major stock holder of Richebourg-Conti.

'Syrah, you've come a long way since your Malibu days and your struggle to survive is admirable. But it has to be over, this playing with your legacy. The only thing that will keep Richebourg-Conti a family business is if you sell Ruy Blas to me. You do that and within three days I will back off my takeover and work something out with Caleb and Paula,' said Ira in his most charming and honeyed voice.

Paula, who was completely out of control with rage, started to rant about how Syrah had ruined everything by not selling to them a year ago. And for the first time ever Syrah wheeled round to face her sister-in-law and told her in a voice that throbbed with anger, 'You are a stupid, greedy, self-serving woman. Don't you *ever* speak to me like that again or I will see you and Caleb and your family on the streets and that's a promise!' Then she stalked from the room.

It was all but over. Ira breathed in the scent of sweet success. Dealing with the Richebourgs, all three of them was, like taking candy from babies. They simply did not know how to fight. None of them had the least idea what straits he was in. That though he was worth hundreds of millions of dollars he was momentarily cash and credit poor as a result of overextending himself in the Napa Valley. He was having to scratch up a million dollars a day to honour the penalty clause in his contract with the Baron, and that was his prime concern.

He had never imagined Syrah would cling on so tenaciously and it was with great relief that he at last saw

Ruy Blas slipping from her grasp.

Syrah knew when she walked away from Château Richebourg-Conti that she had been beaten. She was devastated. On her return to her vineyard she sat silently for hours, trying to come to terms with the fact that only she could save Richebourg-Conti. Confused as to what to do next, where to turn for advice, how to explain to those who had supported her, given her so much, that she was bailing out, against all she had promised herself she called James. She felt obliged to let him know the turn of events, no matter that they had vowed never to see each other unless their paths should cross by chance. Then she flew to San Francisco to pick up Diana who had been working on a movie there and brought her back to Ruy Blas.

Chapter 14

Diana and Syrah were sitting together in the office of the Ruy Blas winery waiting for James to arrive. This room had been Ethan's hideaway, the place where he had brought his best colleagues and friends. The walls and doors were of pear wood, eighteenth-century and hung with Picasso etchings of his Minotaur series. A Louis XIV Library table was placed in the centre of the room and round it five eighteenth-century high back chairs covered in their original tapestry, Hunting the Unicorn. The only other piece of furniture there was a round marble-topped table of the same period on which stood wine glasses and a pair of crystal decanters.

Diana had been most concerned when Syrah had fetched her from San Francisco. The light seemed to have gone out of her eyes, she was ghostly pale and extremely agitated. Diana's first words to her had been, 'What's gone wrong?'

All Syrah had answered was, 'I've had to break my vow and call James. I'll tell you both all about it when the three of us are together.'

Diana had not pressed her. She knew there was no point. Whatever had happened was obviously too painful for her to have to repeat twice. Syrah's anxiety was so acute that Diana was feeling unnerved, and being in this splendid room that was so personal to Syrah did not help. Syrah rarely brought anyone here. The knock at the door made both women jump.

Syrah cleared her throat and then called out, 'Come in.'

The door opened and James stood framed in it with the sunlight behind him, looking every bit the handsome charismatic man he was. On seeing Syrah across the room, he hesitated, as if he had to balance himself before he could take a step. When he did it was to walk silently towards her. And Syrah? She remained silent and went forward to meet him. But they didn't just meet, they embraced each other, held each other in a hug for several seconds. Diana thought her heart would break, so intense were the feelings they had for each other.

Syrah patted James on the back and broke their embrace. There could be no mistaking the devastation she was feeling. She tried very hard to keep calm and get on with telling them the facts but a voice kept screaming in her brain, 'I can't do this. Why? Why must fate snatch a love like mine and James's away? Why am I always losing what I love? Why must I lose Ruy Blas, this wine cellar, after such struggle and sacrifice and when things are working out here? Why is it never allowed that I should do what I want? My life before Ethan's death was always what I wanted – I want that back!'

Syrah was so distracted by her new world falling down all around her yet again that though she offered them chairs round the table she failed to suggest a bottle of wine or a cup of tea. Instead she leaped directly into telling them exactly what had happened at the meeting with Ira, Caleb and Paula at Richebourg-Conti.

The three of them remained silent for several minutes, trying to absorb all that had been foisted on to Syrah at that meeting. James and Diana knew, although Syrah had not as yet told them, that she was going to sell out to Ira.

James spoke up, 'I would happily raise the money for you to save Richebourg-Conti and keep Ruy Blas but my own vineyard is over-extended, I couldn't even make a dent in the sum needed for a move like that. Although on paper I'm a wealthy man it's only my wife who is cash rich enough to give me the money. I can ask, but she'll never do it. She holds her purse tightly closed. There are a few others I can call on but they're just not in the same financial league as Ira.'

Enraged at Caleb, Paula and Ira, Diana scraped her chair back on the stone floor and stood up to pace the room. 'Syrah, let Richebourg-Conti go down the tubes. Just keep Ruy Blas.'

'I can't do that. I believe Ethan would have wanted me to do whatever it takes to keep Richebourg-Conti in the family. Who's to know? Maybe it's poetic justice that Ruy Blas should be snatched away from me. Could it be my penance for having turned my back on it for so many years, woken too late to my love of the vine?'

'What crap!' declared Diana.

'Say you were to sell out to Ira – can you trust him not to boot out Caleb and Paula and swallow up Richebourg-Conti in one gulp for himself? These events are torture for me because I can't help you rid yourself of Ira. We must think this out, Syrah. While I understand your generosity and your belief that what you are about to do is what your father would have wanted, we have to stand back and get a proper picture of what could happen once you have sold your legacy. Can we trust Ira's word that Richebourg-Conti will remain a family company?' asked James.

'There's no point in agonizing over this. I'll call on my attorney in the morning and sell Ira whatever it takes to save Richebourg-Conti.'

Diana was astonished it should all end with Syrah giving up Ruy Blas. She did not trust Ira to play fair. She knew something had to be done but had no more idea what any more than James did.

In the attorney's office, it was one blow after another, with no room to negotiate. Syrah asked to have a seat on the board of Richebourg-Conti as a condition of her sale to Ira. He flatly refused. She suggested she should sell to Caleb and Paula as insurance that they would have a controlling interest in Richebourg-Conti. Again Ira flatly refused. He was adamant there was only one way a deal could be struck and that was that she should sell outright to him. Syrah settled for a sum of $73 million to be paid immediately. She walked from the lawyer's offices a wealthy but confused woman, miserably disappointed to have lost Ruy Blas and with only a matter of days before she had to vacate her vineyard, once again not knowing where she wanted to go or what she intended to do. She joined James and Diana who were waiting for her in the attorney's ante-room.

They could see just how traumatised Syrah was by this turn of events. Minute by minute she was breaking down in front of them. The year of struggle since Ethan's death, her estrangement from James, the loss of the legacy which had meant more to her than the money she now had, were taking a toll on her. She was emotionally drained.

Diana wanted her to return with Keoki and Melba and stay for as long as she liked at her house. 'I can't do that. Keoki's settled and happy at school, has made new friends, loves living here. No, for the time being, I want to stay here in the Napa Valley.'

Diana saw the expression of relief on James's face. 'Syrah's right, Diana. She's in no fit state to make any decisions. What you need,' he told Syrah, 'is a long rest, time to heal from this traumatic loss, have lots of good times to wipe out the bad ones. Have friends who love and admire you for what you have done here in the Valley. And most important of all not to think about Richebourg-Conti until you are feeling well again and in control of your life.'

Diana could see tears in James's eyes. He turned away from Syrah to hide them. He cleared his throat. Taking both women by the arm, he walked them from the office. He could feel the nervous tremors racking Syrah's body and was frightened for her when she simply stopped talking.

In the car he told her and Diana, 'My barn conversion on the edge of Whitehawk Ridge isn't quite finished but it's habitable and that's where I'm taking you. I'll organise your move and tell Keoki and Melba what has happened. You can all stay there until you're well and strong enough to pick up your life again.'

James was as good as his word. He had never told her about the conversion of the barn. He had done it for her, so that she could move out of the shack on Ruy Blas. But then they had broken up and she'd never had the chance even to hear about his making a home for her on his land.

It was still early afternoon when they arrived at the barn. After finding several rickety wooden chairs and a table and putting them out in the sun, James rounded up a crew of men to help him move Syrah's possessions from Ruy Blas. Melba was swept along by the tide of events. It was she who best understood how distraught Syrah must be. She swung into action and took over the move from the shack while James made calls and organised carpenters before he went to pick Keoki up from school.

James took the boy to his favourite ice-cream parlour. Fondness for James was in the child's eyes. He blurted out, 'I knew you would miss us too much to stay away, no matter what Mom and you told me and the girls about the break up being best for all of us.'

Keoki would have continued with his nine-year-old wisdom had not James told him, 'Keoki, for the moment, never mind the break up. I have some bad news for you. There's no easy way to tell you this so here it is straight. Your mom has had to sell Ruy Blas and the wine cellar.'

'*Never*!' shouted the boy and swept the glass dish filled with ice cream aside. James caught it before it crashed to the floor.

Keoki asked in a hollow whisper, 'Is it true, James?'

'Yes, sadly. She didn't want to but was forced into it by circumstances.'

'She didn't even ask me,' said Keoki, then lowered his head and wept.

James walked him through the ice-cream parlour to his Range Rover and helped the boy on to the seat. There, he wiped the boy's eyes and cheeks with his handkerchief, pulled Keoki to him and told him, 'You aren't going back to Ruy Blas. I'm taking you to Whitehawk Ridge where you and your mom and Melba will be living for the time being in a beautiful barn I've just had converted. It will be a great deal more comfortable than the house you've been camping out in. Your mom and Diana are already there. Your mom's not taking this turn of events well. Ruy Blas and the wine cellar had come to be her life. She needs you Keoki: to hold her hand, caress her brow, talk to her and help her get over this unhappy time. She needs to get her strength back and to have fun. You must not show her how desperately unhappy you are.'

'Is she really bad? Worse than when my grandfather died and we had to sell up and move away from Malibu?'

'Yes, much worse.'

'Worse than when you and Mom broke up?' the boy pressed on.

'Keoki, enough of the questions. She's gone very silent and is simply worn out emotionally. She needs you. You need each other. You're going to stay as long as she likes in the barn until she knows what she wants for the two of you. Can I depend on you to be brave and just love her and be happy to be here in the Valley?'

'I want to see my mom,' the boy told him.

James saw a questioning look in Keoki's eyes. He knew what it was. The boy was silently asking, Are you going to get back together? Will we be what we once were, a family of sorts? That that was so impossible hurt James beyond measure. While he had broken his vow to his wife that he would never pick up with Syrah again, he knew that whatever help he was extending to her now, to be in an intimate relationship was out of the question. Returning to his wife and children had been the only thing he could do.

Syrah struggled with her depression. What appeared to have saved her was the barn. It was lovely and spacious, with glass walls that looked across vineyards and hills. The rush of people to make it comfortable for her came and went and almost immediately Melba had it smelling of her gloriously good cooking. No more beans on toast, they had real money for real food and wine. Keoki kept reminding his mother how much better the barn was than the shack had been.

People were generous and called on Syrah but after a few minutes could see she needed to be alone. It was not as if she didn't realise what was going on. On that very first day when the lorry arrived with their personal things from Ruy Blas, it registered with her how poorly they had been living. When she had owned Ruy Blas it hadn't mattered but now that she was an extremely wealthy woman the sacrifices she had put herself, her child and her friends through pained her. She recognised, it had been passion, a need to survive, love that had driven her. She wanted to weep for no longer possessing those things. All drive and spirit seemed to have died in her and she hardly felt the same person. She was able to step outside herself, watch herself suffering, and that only depressed her more. Every day she would tell herself: Stop! But she could hardly do anything about it. She would sit day after day in the sunshine, under a large straw hat, looking across the valley, her mind empty of thoughts, ideas, desires. She felt like the walking dead and let herself wallow in her sorrow. She needed time to gather her strength, have happy times, put all that had happened behind her.

Diana spent as much time as she could spare from her own commitments with Syrah. She watched her friend's life smashed for a second time in less than two years and could see no way for Syrah to rise again, create another independent and exciting life. Diana was bitter about the loss of Ruy Blas. She could feel Syrah's desperation and her plight as strongly as if they were her own. It was all too unfair, so undeserved. There was an innate goodness and generosity of spirit in Syrah which only her real friends appreciated.

Slowly the days went by then the weeks, and time and distance from what had happened began to heal Syrah. She would not deal at all with Caleb, Paula or Ira. On her instructions her lawyers kept them at bay. She had done everything she could to keep Richebourg-Conti and at a cost to herself she would never forget or forgive. Now she began once more to put her life together.

For the first time since Ethan's death she had leisure and money. She began to fly for fun again. Every day she would go up a little bit higher, for a little bit longer. After several weeks she was packing Diana and Keoki into the bi-plane and they would fly along the coast of California to Mexico or join a rally of vintage aircraft in Arizona. But she never stayed away too long, always wanting to return home to the barn. Her heart still yearned for Ruy Blas and her work and for James's love, though they stayed apart, waving to each other from a distance when their paths crossed on Whitehawk Ridge.

Days after Syrah sold out to Ira, Caleb and Paula realised they had lost control of Richebourg-Conti. Ira struck a deal with the husband and wife team that left them with some money, but only enough to keep a roof over their heads. At a price, they had to give up all rights to Richebourg-Conti and that included the family château.

Ira gave way on one thing: he would not make public any details of their loss.

There were, of course, rumours abounding and though Diana had remained, as she had wanted to be, in the background as the secret investor, she was privy to information about Ira and his dealings in the valley. When she heard that he had gone against his word to Syrah and there was no Richebourg at the helm of Richebourg-Conti she did not tell her friend, concluding it would only cause Syrah more distress. Diana knew Ira too well. No appeal to him on the Richebourgs' behalf would ever work. Once she saw Syrah struggling against her depression and growing stronger every day in spite of the pain, Diana began distancing herself. She was leaving her friend and Keoki to work out their emotionally tortured lives.

Syrah and Keoki had been like family to Diana. She loved Syrah as a sister, liked her as a friend. She was loyal and true, courageous and full of life. Her bad luck and the blow she, and now all the Richebourgs, had been dealt by Ira began to eat at Diana's soul and her passion for fairness and justice sprang into action. She was a substantial investor in the Valley and having secretly gone up against Ira and thwarted his land-grabbing, felt *his* greediness to be to *her* advantage. At home in Beverly Hills, she thought about nothing else but that and the proposed movie re-make of A Streetcar Named Desire.

She was to play Blanche Dubois, while in her personal life a plan seemed to be coming together, devious and daring. She felt she had nothing to lose and everything to gain. She was, after all, an actress.

Her first move was to arrange to be at a dinner party where she knew Ira had been invited. She agonized over what to wear and finally settled on an Yves St Laurent black dinner dress she had worn when she received a Bafta Award in London. Around her neck was a diamond choker that Ira had bought her many years before and on her ears square-cut diamonds of considerable size that he had given her when she had won her first Oscar. Her long shapely legs were encased in the sheerest of black silk stockings and on her feet she wore black lizard high-heeled shoes.

Ira found her irresistible: beauty as hot as it was cold, sexy to the extreme, aloof rather than arrogant, and with a face that could make angels sing. When she entered her hostess's house, all went quiet for a few seconds. Diana George had the sort of star quality that did that to people. Several guests gathered round her but not for long. Ira pushed his way forward and claimed her for his own.

'You look dazzlingly beautiful,' he told her, and kissed her on the cheek.

He never left her side but had to tolerate other people joining them. Diana was witty and charming, and Ira wondered how he had been so foolish as to let her walk out of his life. Her wit was dry, her charm never overbearing, and she carried an air of humility about herself and her achievements that was enchanting. All this Ira observed as he stood next to her, drinking champagne and remaining completely unaware that she was flirting with him: a touch to his hand, a smile, the gentle caress of his cheek with the back of her hand.

The room was buzzing about them with rumours of a reconciliation. The hostess dashed into the dining room and switched the seating arrangements to place Diana next to Ira.

Once seated, the couple began to chat in earnest. Ira asked after Syrah and they spoke of her only briefly because they were more interested to tell each other about the loss they had felt on becoming estranged from one another. Their reconciliation was a very public one: gossip columnists who could rarely find anything to write about Diana made the most of it. The *paparazzi* caught them out looking dewy-eyed at one another and sold the photos to the *National Enquirer* and the newspapers.

The following days for Diana were filled with flowers and presents from Ira. He was courting her once more. There were still vestiges of the man she had loved and admired for so long, just a spark. But was a spark enough? she had to ask herself. Ira was in the best of moods. On top: reaping the rewards he had plotted and planned and gambled for, including the woman he wanted to marry on his terms. It had taken only one night of sex with Diana to convince him she wanted him back just as much as he wanted her.

They were in the bedroom of his Malibu house. He

could make love to Diana as no other man could. She realised that orgasms achieved with Ira were an ecstasy unlike any other form of bliss. Orgasm for Diana was one of the miracles of life. As for Ira, he could never get enough of her. No matter how often she came, he wanted her to come again. He adored her the most when she was faint with coming, near to death in her erotic pleasure. He never stopped fucking Diana until she begged him to, until every fantasy of sexual depravity had run its course.

She begged and wept, not with pain but acute pleasure, and they came together and then he held her in his arms and asked, 'Will you marry me?'

'Still on your terms: total freedom, other women?' she asked.

'Yes,' he boldly answered.

'And what about Syrah? I've seen you lust after her. I could not abide you cheating on me with my best friend,' she told him with sadness in her voice.

'Listen, my darling, my heart, Syrah was an option that became an obsession. Sure, there's an attraction between us and in my sexual fantasies I still imagine that one day we will have a liaison. But that's only my imagination and I promise you, if you marry me, that's where it will stay. I love you, Diana, I always have. I want you for my wife, to be the mother of my children, you've always known that. Just as you have always known the other women meant nothing to me compared to you. Marry me. Name your conditions, and if I can meet them honestly, I will.'

'I have to think about this, Ira,' she told him.

'What's to think about? Say yes, and think about it later,' he pressed.

'Give me twenty-four hours,' she told him, sliding on top of him, and they kissed deeply. She nibbled on his nipples then bit into them and kissed her way down his body. Slowly, deliberately, she took him into her warm, silky smooth mouth and caressed him with her tongue, sucked him deeply, subjugated him and his desire to come to her will.

Chapter 15

That first phone call from Syrah to Diana after the dinner party and the newspaper photographs of her and Ira together had been especially difficult for Diana to take. Syrah came directly to the point. 'Tell me it's not true you are reconciled with Ira?'

'It is,' replied her friend.

'How could you go back to him? He's more monstrous than ever. I honestly believed you were over him. Never mind what he's done to me, remember what he's done to you in the past.' Bitterness and anger dripped from Syrah's every word.

'That's the past. I don't want to talk about it or Ira and my relationship with him. It's too complex. We'll talk about it another time. You have enough to think about without my love-life to deal with. You won't talk me out of what I'm doing. Please support me in this.'

The two women had not spoken since they had had that conversation. Things were moving so fast with Diana and Ira there had been little time to think about Syrah.

Diana was awakened one morning by a kiss from Ira

and a reminder, 'You said you would give me your answer. Tomorrow at breakfast?'

'Yes, tomorrow, first thing in the morning,' she told him flirtatiously and then he was gone, flying to Seattle for a meeting. As soon as she heard his car being driven away, Diana called Syrah.

Her friend's first words once she recognised Diana's voice were, 'I'm sorry about the other day. You being back with Ira was just a shock for me.'

'Syrah, can you fly down here for a late lunch? I must talk to you, make you understand that Ira has everything I want and we'll both have to live with that.'

A car was waiting for Syrah when she landed her plane. She was excited at the thought of seeing Diana. She had been miserable at the idea that her friend was back with Ira. It was all wrong and she was certain that Diana was just as aware of that as she was.

A great couturier had once said, 'Women do not dress for their men, they dress for women.' That was the first thing Diana thought when she walked from the house to greet Syrah. Never had either woman looked more beautiful nor so underdressed as they did now. Syrah in a white silk collarless blouse and a pair of blue jeans; Diana in pale silver-grey wide-legged cotton trousers and a smock of the same material. The two women kissed in a greeting that should have been easy and loving and was not.

It was in fact so strained that as they walked through the garden they could only speak of mundane things.

At the table Syrah nervously said, 'We can't just hedge round talking about you and Ira.'

'No, we can't. I'm going to marry him, Syrah. I wanted you to be the first to know, even before him.'

'You can't be that stupid, Diana! What possible reason could you have for marrying him? And don't insult my intelligence and tell me because you love him or the sex is great!' exclaimed Syrah.

'Don't do this, Syrah. Be happy, not jealous because James can't come through to make a life with you.' The moment Diana uttered these words she wanted to bite her tongue, rush round the table and hug her friend to her to try to explain her decision to marry Ira. But that was impossible.

'That's cruel if probably true, though it was the last thing on my mind. And what about what your husband-to-be did to me and my family? Will you be able to wipe that out of your life with Ira? I think not! This is the end of our friendship. You write me off as a friend if you marry him. This man you want for a husband and the father of your children who only a matter of days ago wanted *me* for sex, who said if I played my cards right he might in time marry *me*. You've picked real husband material there! Diana, you're breaking my heart.'

Syrah walked away from the table, devastated. She had been betrayed by her best friend. She walked away from the house, not quite believing that the long-time friendship between them was broken. That afternoon Diana waited for the telephone to ring, to hear Syrah's voice uttering an apology. It never rang. There was never an apology nor any good wishes from her. Diana was unnerved by what had passed between them and sad beyond measure.

That evening she slept at Ira's Malibu house. She was sitting on the beach in front of his drawing-room windows when he arrived the following morning. He took her by surprise, coming up behind her and placing a kiss on the top of her head. His lips grazed her cheeks. Following him two house staff carried a table set for breakfast and two chairs.

'If it's *yes*, you get breakfast,' Ira told her.

'And if it's no?' she asked, a smile on her lips.

'That's not possible. You love me too much. Marry me and I'll give you anything you want for a wedding present.'

'If I marry you, I lose my best friend. Syrah wants nothing to do with us. I'm really angry with her for not being happy for me at the most thrilling time of my life. What I've waited for, always dreamed of,' she told him as she rose from the beach chair and slid her arms around his waist, pressing against him. Something happened in that embrace, Diana sensed he was falling deeply in love with her, out-of-control in love. It overwhelmed her.

'Then I can take it that is a *yes*?' he asked, a smile on his face.

'Yes, I will marry you, and would have married no other,' she told him.

Ira swept her off the sand and into his arms. He

caressed her, kissed her lips and then her face. He laughed and shouted to passers by: 'She said yes! She said yes!'

They were both laughing as he swung her round and round. 'You've made me feel like the luckiest man on earth. You won't regret this. I'll make you happier than we have ever been. I was so afraid you were going to say no. That Syrah would talk you out of happiness.'

Ira pulled Diana down to the sand and on to his lap, kissed her and stroked her hair. 'We've come a long way, you and me, girl. Now I want to put the world at your feet. You deserve nothing less. Let's get married as soon as possible. Big wedding or little wedding?'

'Little wedding, large reception,' she told him, and returned his kisses and caresses.

Diana had overwhelmed him. She now sensed what he had always claimed to be true, that she was the other half of himself. Once he'd committed himself instinct told Diana he would never stop falling in love with her.

Ira interrupted her thoughts. 'I meant what I said before. I want to give you a wedding present, a gift just for you. Something so spectacular every woman will envy you for it. Something big and impressive that no one else can have.'

Diana kissed his ear then whispered into it, 'I choose the deeds to Ruy Blas and Ethan's wine collection. That's not being too greedy, is it?' she asked and kissed him again only this time more deeply.

'You see yourself as a mistress of a small but great vineyard?' he asked, amused by her choice.

'No, dear, not mistress but owner of something rare and beautiful as well as your wife.'

'That would hurt Syrah. Is this some sweet female revenge because she had a thing for me and tried to talk you out of marrying me? I confess it's a delightful revenge and one I approve of. The deeds are yours, my bride. I'll say one more thing. If I've taught you anything in our years together it was never to sell yourself cheap. Now I will be marrying a great actress, the most delicious of lovers, and a financially independent woman. I like it. Yes, I like it,' and Diana kissed him and wept tears of joy.

She told him, feeling she was floating five feet above the ground, 'This is the happiest day of my life. I will always love you for asking me to marry you, and for presenting me with such a terrific wedding present.'

Ira thought that he had never known what happiness was until now. He could not remember having this special something he was feeling that moment with Diana. To be loved as she was loving him was life itself. The deeds she asked for? He would have given her more than that. He was able to sign them over to her because under the terms of his arrangement with the Baron, Ira owned the title to the vineyards. For a fleeting moment he thought about Syrah. He knew he would on occasion still think about her. Their attraction for each other had never been resolved. She had chosen James over him and sexual rejection was always tough for Ira to handle. If it were possible, he loved Diana more for wanting Syrah's legacy and getting it. He smiled over his own final revenge on her.

Only after Syrah returned from her lunch that never was with Diana did she realise how desperate and alone she felt. That what Diana had said in anger was partly true. She wanted a stable life with the man she loved, to build a future with James and their children. She questioned what she had left? Her son and flying, up and away above the mayhem of life. To feel the wind in her face and to soar like a bird or a butterfly. And that she concluded was still a great deal. For several days she and Keoki fell back on barnstorming: a dozen aerobatic events in one small town or another. The jolly camaraderie of men and women with their vintage flying machines distanced her from Diana's treachery, James's fractured love, and the wine world. Taking Keoki with her and making a fun life for them both helped heal over their wounds, made them stronger people. They returned to the Napa Valley and the barn and began to talk seriously about their no longer being poor and just how wealthy they had become. How extravagant they could afford to be. But as the days passed Syrah and Keoki never did go on the shopping spree they had promised themselves. Nor did they hold a large party for their wine friends, or even look for another house, a place where they could live permanently. Those things simply did not answer the call of their hearts.

Only a few weeks had passed since Syrah had sold out to Ira and people found it remarkable that she was, in a fashion, overcoming her disappointment, the deep depression she had slipped into. There were still any number of 'if onlys' that might have saved her and kept her Ruy Blas. But somehow these good people, who had only an inkling of the treachery used against her to make her give up her legacy, could not accept that life would not turn around for Syrah Richebourg.

It began with a pounding on the barn doors at three o'clock in the morning. Syrah and Melba arrived at the door at the same time, Keoki following sleepily behind. It was a warm but windy night and when they opened the door to find Henri Chagny and Blackwolf standing there with James's daughters, the breeze whirled through the house. There were hugs and kisses all around. Betsy and Carrie looked confused but by no means unhappy. They trotted off to Keoki's room as if they were at a pyjama party.

Filled with anxiety and foreboding, Syrah asked, 'James? Is he all right?'

'James is fine. It's Katherine, she's been killed in an automobile accident on the coast road to San Francisco.' Blackwolf explained. 'The children don't know. He called me and asked me to bring them to you and say nothing to them as yet. He is with the police where the accident occurred. There'll be a scandal. She was with a young man who has survived. I don't know anything more. Is it all right for the children to be here?'

Syrah's first reaction to the news of Katherine's death was one of grief for the woman and her children. The pain that Katherine had caused so many people when she was alive was forgotten. But at what cost. Two little girls would be traumatised by a mother's death. Syrah placed her hands over her face and wept from sadness and relief for James, his children and herself.

At midday on the following day James arrived at the barn. He looked distressed and pale as he walked into Syrah's open arms. His first thought was for his children. After calling them, together with Keoki, he calmly told them of their mother's death. The girls took the news as was expected, badly. It took several days for Melba, Keoki and James to comfort them. Betsy and Carrie had chosen to go back to their own house and asked Syrah, Melba and Keoki to go with them. As it had always been with James, his girls wishes came first and as awkward as it might look, moving the woman he loved in with them, he could not have cared less.

Katherine Whitehawk left many surprises behind her. Stories of her disturbed mind and complex personality that James had tried to keep quiet for his children's sake were now aired openly. He had been the last to know of the scenes she'd made in public; the string of lovers, mostly rough trade, she'd commanded. All so hurtful for James, so embarrassing if his children were to find out. All their married life she had used him as a front while she bought her lovers and disposed of them when she was bored. This petite beauty of high social standing had, even in death, cheated her husband.

The will was a further surprise to James. It had been

made more than a decade before when she had left her entire estate to him and had never subsequently been changed. Katherine's threat to destroy their children's love for their father was real enough but using the changing of her will as a weapon to keep him from divorcing her had never really been an option because she knew that money meant nothing to James. It had been just another form of torture for her to use against him.

Now that they were all living under the same roof, the trauma of recent events seemed to haunt James. He could not get over fate having treated them so unfairly. Too late he was wealthy enough to have saved Syrah's legacy and Richebourg-Conti for her.

Sadness pervaded the house and affected them all until the two girls began talking openly about their mother, acknowledging her in some way every day until she became a part of their past that would not be forgotten but a presence that had nothing to do with their lives now in any negative way. Within a matter of days rather than weeks the two families were living together as one.

Nothing had changed between James and Syrah. Their love was stronger, more fulfilling than ever. It quite overwhelmed them. James and she had been through enough when Katherine had been alive, they saw no need now that they were both free to marry, not to do just that and get on with their lives. He asked her. She accepted.

To marry the man she loved and create a large and happy family for their children – a wish that could now be granted. Yet Syrah felt insecure. She was still bruised and battered from the last year of her struggles to stay alive and change her life. Psychologically, even physically, she did not feel fully recovered. Suddenly she found that she had to come to terms with her anxiety about marriage: domesticity on a full-time basis, a male figure coming into her and Keoki's life permanently. Would it upset her son at last to have a father in his life? The boy's happiness, his security? Would he be able to cope with having to share her with James?

Her anxiety was obvious to everyone in the house. It was swiftly brought out into the open and batted around. They were all piled into the Range Rover: the children were to be dropped off at school, Melba to the market, James to his winery. Syrah playing chauffeur when Keoki announced, 'I'm speaking for the girls and me, Mom.'

There were giggles from Carrie and Betsy. Keoki hushed them up and carried on. 'We feel, if it's all right with you, and if you can stop looking for something to agonize over, you should marry James. We agree you're much better and happier with him and us than without him and us. You see, we like living altogether under the same roof and want to be a real family. One with a mother and a father. That's about it, isn't it, girls?' asked Keoki.

A resounding 'Yes!' issued from the two girls as they jumped from their seats to throw their arms around Syrah's neck and kiss the back of her head.

James was the last to leave the Range Rover. Before he climbed down, she told him, 'The children are right, they want what you and I want so let's get on with the wedding. Quiet, just the family, and a big party afterwards. We deserve it.'

All that day Syrah felt as if a great weight had been lifted off her shoulders. Her strength seemed miraculously to have returned. She was ready to cope with life and all it could throw at her. Her mind was suddenly crystal clear. Her pride seemed to be the only obstacle left to overcome and that was linked with the loss of Ruy Blas and Diana's betrayal of her by loving the devilish Ira.

She could not bear to be saved yet again by anyone, least of all by the man she loved and was about to marry and who had already done so much for her. A feeling of having been through too much, that she had gone too far to fail herself and Ethan as she had done, took her over. This new turn of events – James free to marry her, a road open for them to be happy together for the remainder of their lives – seemed to have shocked her into action. Immediately she knew what she had to do. She must find a way to get back the family's vineyards, complete what she had set out to do – becoming a Master of Wine Ethan would have been proud of, run her vineyard and produce a wine he would have admired. She needed a plan.

She spent an enormous amount of time going over a list of questions with her lawyer and then mulled over the answers. That evening there seemed a new kind of gaiety about her that was infectious. The children were aware of her being once again the Syrah they had first met and James sensed a new excitement about her. At the dinner table Keoki announced, 'Watch out world, my mom is back.'

She broke into peals of laughter and told them 'I've let myself be beaten by circumstances but I have not laid down and died. I'm going to marry your dad, girls, and you, Keoki, can have James as the man in our life, even call him Father if the girls don't mind. And I'm going after Ruy Blas, the wine cellar and then Richebourg-Conti.'

She received a standing ovation and they all drank champagne. That evening after the children went to bed, James and Syrah slipped out of the house and drove to the barn. There they made love and a new and fresh kind of lustiness came into their erotic couplings. Neither wanted to hold back, both wanting to experience those moments of ecstasy where they soared into sexual oblivion, orgasm to die and be reborn in.

After a night of unimaginably thrilling sex, James made breakfast for them and they ate it in bed. Over eggs fried in olive oil and served with crisp bacon, and an enormous pot of coffee, he asked, 'Do you have a plan? Remember, whatever you need to do it will come to you, and that includes any money or help I can give.'

'My plan? God, does that sound good! Ruy Blas and the wine cellar first. I'm certain that's right. Ethan always said they were the keys to his kingdom and he was never wrong. I must get Ruy Blas and the wine cellar back before I go after Richebourg-Conti. So far that's all I have as a plan,' she told James.

But that wasn't quite true. Instinct had told her to make an appointment to speak with the lawyers who had drawn up Ethan's will and who still kept all his personal business and private papers. Syrah had instructed them to go through the old deeds of Ruy Blas and to examine them for any detail that might help her to get back the vineyard.

Several days later the lawyers suggested she come to see them. Something had indeed been found. The moment she entered the conference room, she could sense the excitement round the table. They were fighting with her for the sake of the Richebourgs and in particular for Ethan.

Baskin Coolidge chaired the meeting. Syrah immediately noticed the glint in his eyes, the positive attitude. 'Something very interesting has surfaced from those old deeds,' he told her. 'We have discovered that Ruy Blas and the Richebourg-Conti vineyards were planted on Yurok Indian land sold to the Richebourgs on the condition that it, and any establishment or cultivation of the land remained in Richebourg family ownership or reverted back to the original owners.

'Any sale would be null and void unless it was to a Richebourg or the Yurok tribe. The original price was a sum of money plus a yearly tariff of one-fiftieth of a percent of the profits from the vineyard. It was paid to the tribe through a holding company set up in France by the original Richebourg purchaser.

'Had you not insisted that we search back to the original deed we would never have made this discovery. Here, my dear Syrah, is the loophole you so desperately need. Your sale to Ira Rudman is illegal and the continuity of payments to the holding company for more than a century, in fact until the present day, is, we believe, a case to build on. You sold Ruy Blas without knowing of the clause in the original purchase agreement. Was Caleb aware of the original deed and clause?'

'Instinct tells me that he wasn't, but Ethan was and kept it a secret. What did he fear? Maybe not Caleb but probably Paula.'

'I knew your father well, Syrah. Honour would demand of Ethan that no one should manipulate him, wheel or deal him, out of the original agreement,' said Baskin Coolidge.

Syrah sat silently for a few minutes and then told the men round the table, 'I knew my father better than anyone. I know why he kept that information from Caleb and Paula. Ethan enjoyed giving back something to the land, in this case in the form of a tribute to the tribe who originally occupied it.'

One of the lawyers, Wendell Corby, rose from his chair and addressed the group. 'Once we found this extraordinary oversight of the original deed, we took it upon ourselves to get our accountant to try and trace the funds paid to the holding company. It was incredibly easy. Our investigation revealed that the money paid to the tribal holding company each year was listed as "expenses for Richebourg land conservation". Neither Caleb, Paula, nor Ira Rudman's accountants thought to question this expenditure, obviously having considered it necessary maintenance for the vineyards.'

Syrah focused on what these men were trying to tell her. Her heart swelled with relief for the way she had picked herself up, dusted herself off, and gone after what was rightfully hers. She felt flushed with happiness, she had a fighting chance. Looking round the table she could see on their faces looks of respect and admiration for her and sat that little bit taller in her chair.

'What's my first move?' she asked.

Once more Baskin Coolidge took over. 'Syrah, we suggest you should report your oversight to the district attorney at once. Since ignorance is no excuse for breaking the law, you must be seen to be using the law to make good your mistake. You must convince the district attorney that, having learned you had done something illegal, you are offering to return the money Mr Rudman paid you for Ruy Blas. I am sure the district attorney will agree with this firm that Mr Rudman will have to play along since if he doesn't Ruy Blas, by law, reverts to the Yurok Indian tribe. In that case Mr Rudman will be left without his money or the vineyard, though he may go for prosecuting you for fraud.'

'That's your advice?'

'Yes, confirmed Baskin.

Chapter 16

It had been a private wedding and a very public reception. Ira was thrilled by all the fuss, Diana was not. Ira made capital in every way he could on the publicity the event generated. Diana knew that she was giving, probably, the best performance of her life.

Now firmly established as Mrs Ira Rudman, the deeds to Ruy Blas and the wine cellar transferred to her, and in the full knowledge that Ira was besottedly in love with her, Diana was now ready to confront her husband with some home truths. She dressed in what she called her movie star chic look that she knew Ira adored and was always titillated by and went to his office in downtown Los Angeles to surprise him with a visit. She brushed past his secretary and was through his office door before the young woman could announce her arrival.

Diana walked in on Ira chatting up a young, very young, blonde beauty. Embarrassment was not one of Ira's vices. He smiled widely on seeing Diana. He leaned back in his high leather chair and roared with laughter then introduced the two women to each other and suggested the younger one leave while he dealt with his wife.

'She's no one. Just my old habit of chatting up any pretty face. You know me. This is a surprise, you coming without calling. There's a bit of a pun there,' Ira told his wife.

'There's no need to cover up what I just saw, I never expected otherwise,' she told him as she sat down on a chair opposite.

The smile slowly slipped from Ira's face. Never a stupid man he detected at once the edge to Diana's voice, the coldness he had forgotten she was capable of and he had not seen once since their reunion. Fear gripped his soul. He tried to overcome it.

'Don't be angry. I'll take you to lunch, show us off to the world,' he suggested.

'No, I think not. I merely dropped in to say goodbye, Ira. I'm walking out on you and this sham of a marriage. Consider it a little vignette that was written, produced, directed and acted by me. A playlet of pure revenge for the years of humiliation you caused me when I was deeply in love with you. There are other reasons why I am unforgiving when it comes to you: the pain you have caused Syrah by stripping her of her legacy, and the small wine growers you so ruthlessly tried to take advantage of in order to take control of the Napa Valley.

'There are some things you should know. You will never turn the Valley into an Ira Rudman condominium dream machine. I went up against you and have been buying every small vineyard you were after. And now I have Ruy Blas and Ethan's wine cellar, I intend to sell them back to Syrah,' she told him.

'You're making all this up? It's not a good joke, Diana. In fact, it's a dangerous one. You don't know who you're playing with,' he warned her.

'That's why all this has happened, because I *do* know who I'm playing with,' she told him, and rose to her feet.

'You love me!' exclaimed Ira.

'Now *that* was a piece of acting worthy of an Academy Award. I loved you just long enough to get Syrah's legacy back for her. Oh, and I think I did it for Ethan and Keoki too. And we mustn't forget the satisfaction of beating you at your own game,' said Diana.

His last words as she walked away from him were, 'You vengeful bitch! You want a fight, you'll get a fight. I'll go after Ruy Blas and the wine cellar through the courts if I have to. You can't begin to imagine the lies I'll tell to get what I want.'

Once more she turned to face him before she went through his office door. 'Oh, yes, I can. That was always our problem.'

Much to Syrah's consternation Diana was insisting on talking to her. It was James who suggested she could afford to be magnanimous and take the call. 'A friendship such as you two have had shouldn't die over a man,' he told her. Syrah took the call.

The moment that Diana heard her voice, she started in with, 'Now hear me out. It has never been as you presumed. I did *not* fall in love with Ira and betray you. I *never* intended to make a life with him. Let's just call it a short scene of sweet revenge, a balancing of the books. Please, Syrah, I must see you. There are too many things unsaid between us, and some that never should have been said at all.'

It was James who met Diana at Blackwolf's air strip. She had chartered a bi-plane and pilot from one of Syrah's flying friends. Seeing James, his wide smile and enthusiasm for her being there, told her it had been worth all the plotting, scheming, lies and little deceits. They kissed, James placed an arm round her shoulders and they walked to his Range Rover. Waiting in the car was Syrah. The look that passed between the two women was proof enough that they still loved each other, could work on forgiveness. Yet, as they drove away from the air field, their meeting was awkward, Syrah still feeling the pain of being deceived and let down by her once great friend.

A few miles from Blackwolf's vineyard there was a small inn famous for its wine and luscious tapas which seemed never to stop arriving. There they stopped and sat at a table set on a stone promontory that appeared to be hanging over the vineyards below and for as far as the eye could see.

It was Diana who started. 'I have a great deal to say, and an even greater number of things to explain. Let me begin at the beginning. I wanted to save Ruy Blas and the wine cellar from Ira's clutches and exact some revenge in the process for the years of pain he caused me in the name of love. Then it struck me that his greed should be made to work for me. How to do that? None of what I am about to tell you is very nice, but nice had to be left behind when I made up my mind to get your legacy back for you. I plotted it beautifully, executed it brilliantly and my performance was perfect. First I had to make Ira fall in love with me all over again, then I would marry him and insist on your legacy as my wedding present. Revenge on you for not accepting my marriage to him, or so he thought. I didn't dare take you in on my plan because I knew you would never allow me to make such a sacrifice for your sake. Besides, I was only ninety-nine percent sure I could get away with it. The cost in emotional terms was terrific. I never dreamed you would toss our friendship away over my move to marry Ira.'

'I should have guessed you were up to something. But you could have given me a hint,' Syrah told her.

'I didn't dare for fear you might talk me out of this huge gamble.'

The two women stood up and embraced one another and knew they were back in each other's lives again. There followed a lengthy discussion about Syrah's sale to Ira being unlawful. They and James agreed that there would be endless court battles with him over the issue.

'There's only one thing to do. I'll go through with returning Ira's money and you sell back my father's legacy to me,' suggested Syrah.

'Hey, where are you going to get the money? OK, you

have the funds to pay off Ira but then you're broke again. It cost me nothing. Let me just give you Ruy Blas and the wine cellar?' suggested Diana.

They finally came to an agreement which James thought was a double guarantee that Ruy Blas was Syrah's. One was the unlawful sale to Ira, and the second Syrah's purchase of the same property from Diana. The sale was agreed for a peppercorn. The three of them remained in the small inn for hours working out a plan to go forward now that Syrah had back the legacy. James offered financial support but much to his and Diana's amazement Syrah rejected it.

'This enterprise of clawing back Richebourg-Conti is going to take vast sums of money. I think I know where I can get some of it. I could never have come so far without you two but from now on I must try to do this alone, my way. I hope you both understand how important that is to me? No more crutches, no more advice, no more sacrifices.'

There was about Syrah a new kind of power and control. She showed a maturity, clear thinking, a sharp business sense that James and Diana found admirable. There seemed to be excitement in the air, as if the atmosphere was drenched in adrenaline.

As late afternoon settled in Syrah said, 'The good times have begun to roll and I need to be dressed for them. A shopping spree is what's called for. I need some seriously elegant clothes, power dressing to suit my ambitious intentions.'

* * *

That very day, while Syrah and Diana were shopping, the newspapers were full of the news that Richebourg-Conti was now owned by the French firm Château Brilliant Vivier after a hostile take-over. While the Napa Valley was reeling from this news, it meant nothing to Syrah except another way forward. Once she had her wardrobe and her lawyers and accountants had got together and mapped out her plan, she wasted no time. Leaving James and Diana with Melba and the children, she rented a small jet and flew it to San Francisco, having called ahead and asked Sam Holbrook to take her to dinner.

This was to be the first time they had seen each other since they split and Syrah had returned to James. Female vanity took her over as she dressed for the evening. She wanted Sam to think her as much a beautiful woman as a business person. It seemed important to her not to be seen as too ambitious and controlling a female but rather a lady protecting her birthright and the family company. A beautiful, clever and wise creature with a good brain in her head and a will of iron.

They met in a grand restaurant in San Francisco. The attraction between them was as strong as ever. They were extremely pleased to see each other. Sam had often wondered about his decision to walk away from Syrah and choose to be just good friends. Now, seeing her, he knew that he had been right.

'Are you still with James?' he asked after greeting

her with a kiss on each cheek.

'Yes. We'll marry as soon as I straighten out a few details,' she told him.

That news did nothing to dampen their evening together. Genuinely interested in one another, they each brought the other up to date with what had been going on in their lives. Sam was astounded to hear of the terrible times she had gone through, the courage she had shown in always doing what was right, what Ethan would have wanted her to do. The twists and turns of fate might surely have killed off a lesser woman. He loved her more for her will to survive and prosper.

Finally, over coffee, he asked, 'What do you want from me, Syrah?'

'Money, an investment. My intention is to own all the Richebourg-Conti vineyards and wineries again. My first step on that road is to return the money Ira paid me for the Ruy Blas vineyard and Ethan's wine cellar. You already know that Diana George has sold me the deeds to them for a peppercorn, so I own them twice over. But am left with no cash reserves. I want you to lend me the money I need in exchange for a forty percent share of my legacy, with me retaining the right to buy you out over a period of time. A payment that would be agreeable to us both and financially advantageous to you, Sam, would be part of the deal.'

For the next hour and a half they discussed the pros and cons of why he should or should not invest in Ruy Blas. The more they talked and he heard Syrah's clever plan, the more interested Sam was. Finally he said, 'You've convinced me, let's do it.'

Time was on Syrah's side, circumstances were favouring her. It was difficult to understand exactly why fate had chosen to intervene but she was clever enough not to question that too closely.

The following morning she flew Sam and herself back to Los Angeles and there in her lawyer's offices an agreement was reached and papers drawn up. Nine hours later, the documents signed and with Diana holding an IOU for $50 million and Sam holding a forty percent share of Ruy Blas, Syrah was liquid enough to make a raid on Richebourg-Conti. James arrived and the three former underdogs of the big time wine industry of the Napa Valley went for a celebration dinner with Sam Holbrook.

He was clearly dazzled by Diana, amazed by her loyalty to Syrah, the courage it must have taken and the cunning to have done what she had done out of a deep sense of justice. Syrah's determination to survive and thrive had changed all of these people's lives. But as Sam put it, 'It's not over yet, Syrah. You've got your parcels lined up. Now you have to bring back the prize.'

Syrah felt as hard as steel, as ready to fight for Richebourg-Conti as she would ever be, as she entered the lobby of the Ritz Hotel in Paris. Once checked into the suite of rooms she had taken for herself and her staff, an accountant and two lawyers, she ordered a superb

271

luncheon to be served in the dining room of the suite. Then she bathed and thought hard about the several conversations she had had with Baron Michel de Brilliant Vivier. Feeling secure and determined that she would fly home owning Richebourg-Conti she left her bath, dressed, and very carefully made up her face and did her hair.

The Baron arrived exactly on time as she had guessed he would and by the look on his face she could see he had acquiesced to her wishes and not said anything to his partner Ira Rudman, believing as she had promised that his silence would be advantageous to him.

This was the first time the Baron had met Syrah. He had been intrigued by her phone calls and was now enchanted by her vivacity and chic, her perfect French and instantly recognisable sensual appeal. Though from the moment he entered the room the Baron was never off guard, they had a charming and civilised chat about her father, Paris, the Baron's opinion of California.

Within half an hour, Syrah came to the point. She told him, 'I am not a devious person, I am new to the world of big business and takeovers. All of this is hard for me to come to terms with. I don't like being out of my depth so I stay where I am comfortable, putting things on the line and dealing openly. I came here to tell you that a coup has taken place. I am now the owner of Ruy Blas and Ethan's wine cellar.'

'That's a very amusing fantasy, my dear, and quite impossible, I can assure you of that,' he told her.

Syrah rose from her chair and walked across the room

to open a door to one of the outer rooms of the suite. She called in one of the lawyers. Syrah introduced the Baron to Baskin Coolidge who assured him that it was quite true and presented documents of Syrah's proof of ownership plus a copy of the original land deed, explaining the loop hole and how it had been overlooked. The Baron being unable to take this blow at face value or to accept the opinion of either Syrah or her lawyer, she called in the second lawyer and the firm's accountant. For an hour they went over every aspect of the facts presented. A quick and astute man himself, the Baron soon saw that if nothing else the Richebourg girl would keep them in litigation for years. He telephoned his own lawyers and ordered them to the Ritz at once.

He was outraged to think this chit of a girl was about to outflank him in the Napa Valley and told her, 'Without Ruy Blas and Ethan's wine cellar, Richebourg-Conti is much less interesting to me and my American ambitions.'

By eleven o'clock that evening the Baron had had enough of Syrah and her team who kept throwing up illegalities at every turn. The Baron tried to save his position as owner of both Ruy Blas and Richebourg-Conti.

'Syrah, what if I were to assume, which I am not doing, that you and your lawyer's allegations are true? What are the options open to me for sole possession of Ruy Blas?'

'Baron, there is no avenue left to you. You are not a Richebourg,' she told him not unkindly.

Always cool and charming, the urbane Frenchman sensed that it was finished.

Charm, the good life, frivolous chatter had always been a game well played by Syrah. It had after all been her world before Ethan's death. And that afternoon she had played brilliantly. The Baron watched her with admiration. For all her feminine charms he was now able to see her as a clever and ruthless predator who, if given what she wanted might be persuaded to minimise the tremendous embarrassment of his having lost the prize he had so brazenly flaunted. He hoped that he could extract from Syrah sufficient money to cover his enormous financial loss and Château Brilliant Vivier's reputation in the wine industry. The Baron had no doubt that to fight Syrah Richebourg and Ira Rudman in the American courts would be a battle of many years, expensive, scandalous and hardly appealing.

It was nearly midnight when he asked for champagne which was ordered by Syrah and served to everyone in the room. A strange silence settled over everyone. The tension of the last few hours, the dickering and all the fighting seemed to go out of the two principals and their teams. The Baron, sitting on a settee next to Syrah, had only one consideration: the continuity of his French wine empire.

Turning to face her, he told her, 'You are playing a game of what you Americans call hard ball with a master, but I am at least willing to play. What will it take for Richebourg-Conti not to be snatched out from under me and be given to the Yurok tribe?'

Syrah felt a serge of triumph run through her. She held back tears of relief, just prevented herself from shouting with joy for her victory. She gazed into the faces of the people in the room and could see the astonishment on every one of them. Her heart was full of joy and love for Ethan. With great humility, having brought herself under control, she studied the Baron's face.

In a strange way she was grateful to him for being so clever, quick to understand that she was prepared to give a great deal to have Richebourg-Conti for herself, that she was there to negotiate with the Baron rather than Ira for his share of the Richebourg-Conti vineyards and winery.

After another day and a half in Paris, Syrah Richebourg flew from Paris to Los Angeles having achieved the unthinkable: owner of Ruy Blas, Ethan's wine cellar and the Baron's stake in Richebourg-Conti, she was now the major stockholder of all the Richebourg vineyards.

She arrived in California with the Baron. Together they approached Ira with the news that he had lost control of Richebourg-Conti in a bloodless business coup.

Brazenly, before he could shout treachery a second time, Syrah pounded hard on Ira's desk for his attention and in a hard voice took her last, most dangerous, gamble.

'Ira, I will buy you out of Richebourg-Conti for the exact sum it cost you to ruin Caleb and not a penny more,' she told him.

The Baron followed up with, 'I insist you take the

deal offered you, Ira, because if you don't and condemn us all to years of litigation in a case that no one will benefit from, plus ruining a great vineyard, I will have no choice but to label you an embezzler, a liar and a thief, who walks on the edge of respectable business. I have enough proof from my years of association with you.'

It was all over in a matter of hours. At the Beverly Hills Hotel, Syrah changed from her elegant power dressing to a black leather jump suit. In her double-winged vintage Boeing Stearman she flew away from Los Angeles, the owner of debt-ridden Richebourg-Conti and Ruy Blas, Ethan's coveted wine cellar, and with waivers from both the Baron Michel de Brilliant Vivier and Ira Rudman of any right to sue her for fraud over her sale to Ira.

She soared into the air over the ocean at Malibu, flew barrel rolls, dives and spins above the water's edge as it rolled on to the beach, as she had the day Ethan was brought down by a stroke. She felt so different from the person she had been that day. She was aware that she would never again be the same person she had once been. Her perceptions were different, and her passions. This was her second chance and she felt joyful that she could now appreciate the world and life from a different vantage point.

It was late afternoon when she circled Richebourg-Conti and as she came in to land she saw waiting on the ground at the end of the grass air strip a clutch of people waving their arms: Keoki, Melba, James and his girls,

Henri Chagny, Blackwolf, Sam Holbrook and Diana among the dozens of staff from Ruy Blas and Whitehawk Ridge, from Richebourg-Conti and many of the small vineyards she and Diana had helped. Syrah's heart was bursting with pride and love as she pulled up into the air and returned, dipping her wings from side to side as she made her landing.

Objects of Desire

Roberta Latow

*Suppressed passions, secret cravings and erotic fulfilment
come together in this sensational novel of desire*

Married to a world-famous surgeon, and mother of
twin boys, Anoushka Rivers seems to lead a perfect
life. But her erotic nature is suppressed by a man who
does not love her.

Page Cooper has spent a decade longing for a man she
can never have. For three weeks of each year, they
experience the sweet ecstasy of desire, knowing that
it cannot last.

Sally Brown is a good-time girl looking for love.
When she finds it in the arms of Jahangir, a darkly
sensuous Indian prince, her sensuality is awakened as
never before.

Drawn together, these dynamic women explore their
true potential – mentally, physically and sexually. A
liaison with a seductive stranger on board the QE2; an
afternoon of erotic depravity in Paris; a lustful *ménage
à trois* overlooking the Taj Mahal; endless nights and
days of unbridled passion with men willing to submit
to their every desire, exploring fantasies beyond
belief. In their search for new horizons, they find
within themselves a strength and peace of mind more
satisfying than anything else. These women are truly
– Objects of Desire.

0 7472 4866 4

HEADLINE

Forbidden

Roberta Latow

Amy Ross, a celebrated art historian, has had many lovers in her lifetime. Again and again she has tasted the sweet ecstasy of sexual fulfilment and erotic depravity. Now, in her later years, she lives as a recluse, blissfully content in her own isolation, an enigma to her friends and admirers.

But Amy has suppressed the memory of her one secret obsession – her love affair with the artist Jarret Sparrow. Their relationship was beyond belief, her love for him dominated her entire life and took her to the furthest limits of carnal desire. Their feelings were too powerful to control – but their love for each other was ultimately forbidden.

Since their separation, Jarret and his manipulative Turkish friend Fee have seduced numerous women in pursuit of their ambition to conquer the art world. And now Jarret is about to re-enter Amy's life. For all those years, Amy had thought it was over. But is she prepared to rekindle the flames of her desire, and at what price . . . ?

'A wonderful storyteller. Her descriptive style is second to none . . . astonishing sexual encounters . . . exotic places, so real you can almost feel the hot sun on your back . . . heroines we all wish we could be' *Daily Express*

'Latow's writing is vibrant and vital. Her descriptions emanate a confidence and boldness that is typical of her characters' *Books* magazine

'It sets a hell of a standard' *The Sunday Times*

'Explicitly erotic . . . intelligently written' *Today*

0 7472 4911 3

HEADLINE